The BIG BOOK of STORIES FROM MANY LANDS

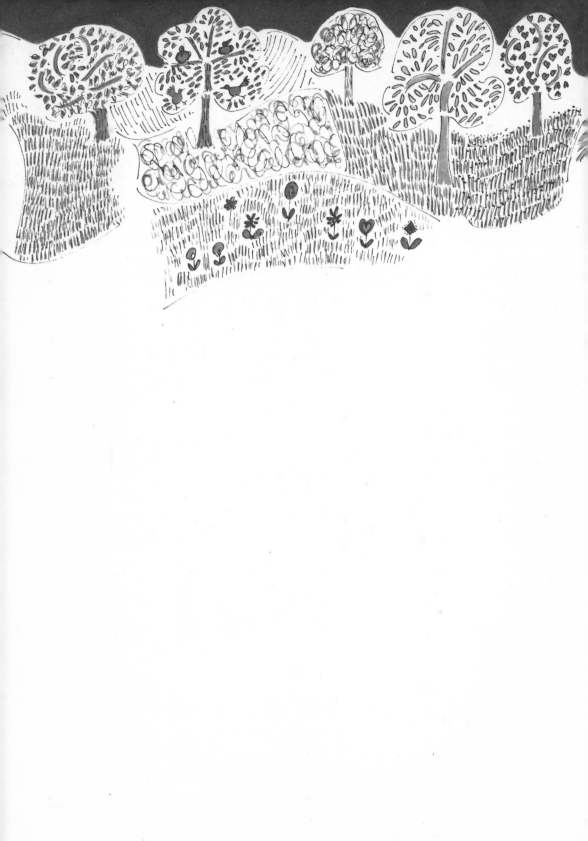

The BIG BOOK of STORIES FROM MANY LANDS

by
RHODA POWER

pictures by
BERNADETTE WATTS

FRANKLIN WATTS, INC.
575 Lexington Avenue, New York 10022, N.Y.

watts
INTERNATIONAL

Originally published in 1931 by Evans Brothers Ltd, London
This edition first published in the United States of America in 1970
by Franklin Watts, Inc, 575 Lexington Avenue, New York 10022, N.Y.
Library of Congress Catalog Card Number: 68–30962
Printed in Great Britain by Redwood Press, Trowbridge
Text film set by Yendall & Co Ltd, London
Illustrations reproduced by Colour Reproductions, Billericay

TO IMOGEN GARRETT

who once asked me why I troubled to write history
when there were such things as fairy tales

Contents

About this Book

Rhoda Power was an eager reader of fairy tales, fables, folklore. This Englishwoman was also a student of Eastern languages, which she learned in part by reading fairy tales. To the despair and amusement of her Russian teacher, she acquired—from the *skazki*—a vocabulary of antique and archaic words not really suitable to everyday conversation.

When, in time, Rhoda Power herself became a teacher, she found that fables and old tales which she had loved as a child proved attractive to a Syrian student whom she was initiating into the English language. And she persuaded this student to tell fairy stories of her own country. Thus *The Shepherd's Treasure* and *Zarifa and the White Calf* came to Miss Power as sort of an exchange gift for English tales.

Other pieces in this book are variations on a theme. She noted, when first her collection of stories appeared in 1920, that people on opposite sides of the ocean, people living very different lives have none the less had similar tales to tell.

Thus, the Algonquin Indians of the United States have a folk tale about *The Hunter Who Married a Star Maiden*, while thousands of miles away a teller of quite different nationality has told a parallel story, the Celtic account of *The Man Who Married a Fairy*.

But perhaps the best are those stories recast with additions of realistic details from the writer's personal experience. Recollecting the high point, the funny twist, the kernel of a story out of Keightley's *Fairy Mythology* or some small volume found in a secondhand bookshop, the author has told the story as it pleased her. Remembering a Spanish

legend about a magic violin that made the judge and jury dance, and thus saved a half-witted beggar about to be hanged for theft, she added herself and her own civilised point of view to a fresh version: "As I did not like tales of half-wits and hanging, the result was *Lazy Carlos and the Enchanted Fiddle*."

For anyone who likes to see how with each age, old-time stories take new forms, this book is a find.

SARAH CHOKLA GROSS,
for the publisher.

What's in the Moon

(English, Maori and African)

Nearly every country has a story about the moon and the shadows on its surface.

The Eskimos say that the moon was once a boy who used to tease his sister so much that she was afraid of him. One night he jumped from behind a tree and said, "Bo!" She did not know it was her brother, and thought that some other boy was trying to frighten her. This made her angry, so she smeared her hands with soot and rubbed them on his face. When it was light she saw the soot on her brother's face, and was so afraid that she ran away. Her brother chased her and they ran so far that they ran into the sky, where the girl became the sun and the boy the moon. To this day you can see the soot which the moon's sister smeared on his face.

The Filipinos say that the sun and the moon were once twins. One day they quarrelled because they each wanted to rule the world. The boy struck the girl and hurt her eye. When he saw what he had done, he was sorry, and he agreed to rule the world by day as the sun and to let his sister rule by night as the moon. But because the brother had hurt his sister's eye, the moon was never able to shine as brightly as the sun.

Perhaps you think that it's nonsense to say there's a man in the moon. Maybe it is and maybe it isn't. Anyhow, there's a story about him.

Once upon a time there was a cross old man who lived with his wife and his dog in a tumble-down cottage at the edge of a wood. He was always bad-tempered and he was always cold.

His poor old wife did her best to keep up a big fire, but the old man did nothing but grumble and shiver. "Brr! Brr! Can't you put on more wood? I'm cold;" and he would huddle up to the fire, warming his hands and complaining bitterly.

It was hard for his wife. The old man never helped her to dig the potatoes or pull up the weeds in the garden. If he went out, he never took his wife for a pleasant stroll and he never stood still to hear the birds singing. He did not even pick the wild flowers. He spent all his spare time gathering sticks to throw on the fire. He did it every day except Sunday, and on Sunday he and his wife put on their best clothes and went to church in the nearest town.

One winter, when the snow lay on the ground and icicles hung from the roof, the old man was colder and crosser than ever. When his wife called to him to get ready for church on Sunday, he refused to move away from the fire, and she was obliged to go by herself.

For a long time the old man crouched over the flames, warming his hands and complaining. Outside, the snow was very deep, and his wife had such a long way to walk to church that she did not come home till the evening.

"Well, man," said she, "it was a beautiful service and I'm sorry you missed it."

The old man turned round crossly. "Did you pick up any sticks? I've burnt nearly everything we've got!"

"Oh man, man," said the old woman, "how could I pick up sticks in this weather? If you don't put on so many, those will last till morning."

The old man began to shake with anger. He pulled his coat off a nail on the wall. He unhooked the lantern and he whistled for the dog.

"I'll get the sticks myself," said he.

"You couldn't go to church in the cold this morning," said his wife, "so how can you go to get sticks this evening? It's colder than ever."

"Bah!" said the old man.

He lit the lantern. He whistled for the dog and went out into the night.

He did not find many sticks. There was far too much snow, and at last he had to go into the woods and cut down a thornbush.

"Show your face, moon," said he crossly, "you're no more use than this lantern. Give me some light, can't you?"

"You shall have all the light you want," said the moon, grinning.

The old man's lantern sputtered and went out. His dog began to howl, and, before he knew what was happening, the old man felt himself being pulled up into the sky.

He clung on to his thornbush and he clung to his dog. He wouldn't let go of his lantern. And, a few hours later, when his wife came out to look for him, she saw him up in the moon.

And that's why the English say there's a man in the moon.

But if you were to tell *that* story to the Maori children who live in New Zealand, they would say, "Pooh! How silly! A man in the moon, indeed! There's a girl in the moon, not a man."

Then they would tell you this story.

Once upon a time there was a girl whose name was Rona. She was very pretty, but not very good-tempered, and she used to get quite cross if people didn't do exactly what she wanted. Well, one night Rona was very thirsty and she wanted some water. Luckily the moon was shining, so she knew that she could easily find her way through the woods to the river. She picked up a jar and crept out of her house. Away she went quite happily, but no sooner had she got into the darkest part of the wood than the moon was suddenly hidden by a cloud, and Rona was left in the dark. She stumbled over a branch and hurt her foot. Oh, she *was* angry. She called out to the moon, "Hi, you! Come out at once."

But the moon took no notice!

Rona looked up and began to make faces at the sky. "You ugly old thing, come out. Do you hear? *Come out,* I say. COME OUT, old white face!"

She stamped her foot and grimaced and shouted.

"You great crosspatch. Don't stay there sulking. Will you come out or——!"

But still the moon took no notice.

Rona stooped and picked up a stone.

Then a queer thing happened. Just as she threw the stone, her feet left the ground and she found herself floating up in the air. Up, up, up she went, struggling and screaming until she had reached the tops of the trees. She caught hold of a branch to save herself, and—*the tree came up by the roots.*

So there was Rona, water-pot, tree and all, floating up into the sky. And she never stopped until she fell back flop! into the moon.

And there she is to this day. At least so the Maori children say.

But if you were to tell that story to an African child he wouldn't believe you. He would say, "A girl in the moon! Rubbish, there's nothing in the moon but an enormous crack, where it once nearly got broken."

And *he* would tell you this story.

Once upon a time there was a little prince who was a spoilt child, and not only a spoilt child, but a *boaster*. One day he was playing in the garden with his friends, and he stuck his head in the air and said, "My father, the king, will give me anything I want." Then one of his friends, who was a little tired of the way the prince always boasted, said, "Well, anyhow, there's one thing he can't give you, and that's the moon."

The prince felt a bit worried, but all he said was, "Oh, indeed! We'll see about that." And he went straight back to the palace and asked his father for the moon.

His father's answer was astonishing.

He said, "Certainly, my dear boy. I'll see about it at once."

Of course, when he heard that, the little prince was delighted, and he became more boastful than ever.

The king was accustomed to giving the prince whatever he wanted, and so he was not at all disturbed by his promise. He sent for his builders and told them to collect all the wood and stones in the kingdom and build a tower which would touch the sky.

The builders set to work. Day after day, week after week they worked. The tower grew higher and higher until, after six months, the chief builder came to the king and said, "Your Majesty, I am ready to bring down the moon."

"All right," said the king, "I'll just come and watch you do it."

"And I'll come too," said the little prince, "wait for me."

Well, they all set out. The chief builder led the way. Then came the

king, and last of all the prince. Up they went, and up! And up and up and up. They climbed and climbed and climbed for twenty days until at last they reached the very top of the tower and found themselves in the sky.

"Bring down that moon!" said the king.

"Ow, ow!" cried the chief builder. "I touched it and it's *hot*."

"Don't make such a fuss," said the king, "bring it down at once."

The chief builder felt a bit nervous. He didn't want to burn his fingers again, but he didn't know how to dislodge the moon, so he just held his breath and gave it a great heave with his shoulder.

And——and a most awful thing happened. He pushed so hard that his shoulder went clean through and and—HE BROKE THE MOON.

He did, really. He made a huge crack in it.

Just as he did this, there was a terrible explosion. The tower burst into flames, and the king, the builder and the prince disappeared in the smoke and were never heard of again.

Ever since *that* day there has been a crack in the moon.

Anna Maria
and the Three Boxes

(Austrian)

Have you seen any of the beautiful boxes they make in Austria?
They come in all shapes and sizes and are intricately carved and
painted. Anna Maria's three boxes must have been very small as
she could put them all into her pocket together. And such small
ones are especially attractive; it is not difficult to believe they have
magic properties.

Once upon a time there was a little girl called Anna Maria. She wore a
blue dress and a black apron with a frill. She was a nice little girl, but
she was really rather *odd;* that is she wasn't an ordinary child. She ate
and slept and ran and jumped and played and did lessons just like
other children. But she wasn't the same. The way she spoke was
different; she always talked in rhyme. She simply couldn't help it.
If you met her in the street on a fine morning and said, "Good
morning," Anna Maria would say,

> "Good day to you,
> The sky is blue!"

or something of that sort. And if it happened to be wet and you met
her going to school, she would shout cheerfully,

> "What a bother! Once again
> I'm getting my feet wet in the rain."

Anna Maria's parents didn't like it very much. They could not understand why their little girl was so different from other little girls, and they did their best to make her stop talking in rhyme. They offered her prizes if she would stop. They promised her extra jam for tea, but it was all of no use. Anna Maria went on talking in rhyme because it seemed she couldn't help it. Her parents thought she must be ill, so they gave her medicine, but that didn't help—Anna Maria only cried,

> "Bring me a basin—*Do* be quick
> This medicine makes me feel so sick."

Then her parents thought she was simply being naughty, so they began to see what punishment would do. They sent her to bed without any supper, but Anna Maria only burst into tears and said,

> "I'm hungry, please
> I want some cheese!"

They put her in the corner, but that did no good. They took away her toys, they "kept her in" after school—but they couldn't stop her from talking in rhyme, and one day, when she had been worse than usual, they smacked her so hard that they really hurt themselves, and all Anna Maria said was,

"You can scold me, you can whip me, you can put me into bed,
    But I can't help saying what comes into my head."

After that they saw that it was no use bothering with Anna Maria, so they shrugged their shoulders and let her be, and she went on talking in rhyme until everyone got quite used to it and took no more notice.

Time passed and Anna Maria led the usual life of a little girl, but a day came when she had an adventure.

It was on her way to school. She was running along quite merrily with the other boys and girls, swinging her school-bag which had her lunch and her books in it, when she saw at the end of the road an old, old beggar. Anna Maria stopped. So did the other children. They

completely forgot their manners and stood quite still and stared with their mouths wide open.

Perhaps they had some excuse, for certainly the old beggar looked most extraordinary. His white hair hung down at the back as far as his heels, and his white beard hung down in front as far as his toes. In his hand he held a piece of plain wood; and if you had gone up to that piece of plain wood and looked at it, you would have seen something written on it—two words—STONE DEAF.

Anna Maria knew how to read, and she felt very sorry for the old man, and wanted to talk to him. "I say," said she to the other children,

> "He can't hear a word, the poor old fellow,
> He's deaf as a post so we'll have to bellow."

She put her hand up to her mouth and shouted in the beggar's ear,

> "Mr. Man, please to tell
> Do you hear me when I yell?"

"Thank you kindly, little lady," said the old man, "I can hear you nicely, my dear, very nicely."

> "Are you hungry? Do you want to eat?
> Would you like some bread or p'raps some meat?"

said Anna Maria. The old man stroked her arm with his thin hands and nodded his head. His eyes began to look very bright.

"Oh, do come *on,* Anna Maria!" said the other children. "We'll be late for school."

"Leave him alone," said one. "You know you're not allowed to talk to strangers."

> "Poor old thing, just look at his rags!
> Let's give him the lunch we have in our bags,"

said Anna Maria. The children edged away.

"Oh, I say, you others. Come on," said a little boy. "If Anna Maria wants to give her lunch, she can. *I'm* going to school."

Off he went and all the others followed, leaving Anna Maria alone with the beggar. She felt a little frightened when she saw the greedy look in his eyes, but she plucked up her courage, opened her satchel and took out something folded in a clean, white napkin. She smiled shyly at the beggar and said,

> "I've got a mother who knows how to bake!
> I'll give you a piece of her best plum cake."

And then and there she handed over all her lunch to the old man.

Then, to her great surprise, the old man took three plums out of the cake, breathed on them and whispered something, and there, before her very eyes, they turned into three little wooden boxes.   .

"Take these boxes," said the old man, "and keep them for three years, and if you're ever in trouble, open one. You'll find something helpful inside."

Anna Maria bobbed a curtsey. She was just going to thank him when, to her great astonishment, she found he wasn't there at all. He'd just disappeared—swish!—like a puff of smoke. Anna Maria rubbed her eyes, peered into all sorts of corners, but he wasn't there. She knew that she couldn't have been dreaming because she still held the three little boxes in her hands, and so, feeling very puzzled, she put the boxes into her pocket and ran as fast as she could to school. Her friends laughed at her when they saw that she had no lunch to eat at playtime, but Anna Maria didn't care. *She* had her little boxes, but she didn't tell, she only said,

> "I wish you wouldn't tease,
> Leave me alone, please,"

and ran home to hide her treasures.

She was a little bit disappointed when she saw that they were empty, but the old man had told her to keep them for three years, so she put them away and thought very little more about them.

Then came her second adventure! She left home and went to work. She was poor, so she found work as a servant in a big house several miles away. She took her clothes in a bundle and her three little boxes tucked away in her pocket, and set out to walk.

For miles and miles she trudged over a long, winding road and through a forest until, at last, she came to the big house. It was quite dark, and Anna Maria was frightened, but when she saw the moon looking at her in a friendly way from behind a tree, she plucked up courage and rang the bell.

For a few minutes she heard the clang echoing through the house. Then there was silence. Anna Maria waited and listened breathlessly. Presently she heard the sound of shuffling footsteps, and a very cross voice asked, "Now then! Now then! Who's there?"

The door opened and there stood a woman with a broom in her hand. "Now then," she said, "why don't you speak when you're spoken to? Don't stand dithering there! Who are you?"

Anna Maria began to cry,

"Oh, dear! Oh, dear! I'm so afraid.
If you please, ma'am, I'm the new maid."

"Oh, indeed!" said the woman. "Come in, then, and be quick about it. Put down your bundle. There. Now set to work and don't snivel. D'you hear me?" And she drove the poor child into the kitchen with her broom, and made her prepare a meal and do all the work of the house before she went to bed.

That night Anna Maria cried herself to sleep, but she cried still more the next morning when her new mistress pushed her into the kitchen and locked the door, saying, "Make me a cake with golden currants. If you don't, you'll have to stay here for seven years." Anna Maria began to sob,

> "Boo hoo hoo,
> What shall I do?"

when she suddenly remembered her boxes. She took them out of her pocket and opened the smallest—and, if you please, out rolled a little cake with golden currants. Anna Maria was so excited that she danced all round the kitchen singing,

> "I didn't mix and I didn't bake
> And yet I've made a currant cake!"

She made such a noise that the woman came in. When she saw the cake, instead of being pleased, she was angry. She shook Anna Maria by the shoulder and said, "You haven't finished your work yet! If you don't make a dress as shining as the sun, you'll stay here for seven years!" She gave the girl a hard whack with the broomstick and went out, locking the door.

But Anna Maria didn't care. She only laughed,

> "I don't mind her shakes and her knocks,
> *I'm* going to look in my second box."

She opened the lid and out of the box she pulled a dress as shining as the sun.

Well, of course, when the mistress came back she was angrier than ever, for she saw that she was never going to be able to keep Anna Maria with her for seven years. However, she said nothing but, "You haven't finished yet. Go into the garden and build me a glass castle

28

as high as a mountain. If you don't, I'll keep you here for twenty years. Now then, be off!" And she pushed Anna Maria outside and locked the door.

The poor girl felt that a glass castle as high as a mountain couldn't possibly be in the third box, which was so small, but she opened it all the same. And what do you suppose tumbled out?

No, not a glass castle, but a tiny little man on a tiny little horse, and they grew and grew and grew until within a few minutes a life-size prince mounted on a white charger stood in front of Anna Maria.

"Why," said he, bending over and kissing her hand,

> "You're the prettiest thing that I've ever seen.
> Come to the palace and be my queen!"

Anna Maria could scarcely believe her ears. He'd spoken in rhyme. When she didn't answer, he looked quite sad.

"Alas!" said he,

> "You hate to hear me talk in rhyme.
> I can't help doing it all the time."

When Anna Maria heard this, a very loving understanding look came into her eyes. She stood on tiptoe and kissed the young man's cheek, whispering,

> "Don't be afraid of speaking, prince.
> Your rhyme will never make me wince."

Then the prince put out his hand and cried,

> "Jump on the back of my good white horse,
> For you're the girl I'll marry, of course."

Anna Maria jumped up behind him and they galloped away, away, away to a far country, where they lived happily and had a dozen children, who always, every single one of them, talked in rhyme.

Imagine! A dozen children all talking in rhyme.

The Hunter
who Married a Star Maiden

(Algonquin Indian)

An Indian hunter, like White Hawk in this story, did not expect to find he had married a star maiden! His wife was an Indian woman, called a squaw. They might have lived in a wigwam made of branches, filled in with moss and lichen, or a sort of tent made of deerskins sewn together; but it is more likely that they lived in a long low house made of tree trunks, with several other families.

They called their baby a papoose, and while they slept on the ground on a buffalo robe or mat, they put it to sleep in a sort of hammock or cradle made of birch bark, padded with moss, and hanging from the roof

Both he and his wife wore tanned deerskin shirts and leggings, and shoes called moccasins, made of soft skins decorated with porcupine quills, dried grass and feathers. Instead of a necklace, his squaw wore the claws of some small animal strung together on the dried sinews of a bear or some other creature which he had hunted and killed. He used the sinews for stringing his bow. His wife and the other squaws dried and cured the skins of all the animals which he and the other men had brought home. They kept the sinews, because they had no cotton then, and when they wanted to make clothes they pierced holes in two skins and joined them together by pulling the dried sinews in and out and knotting the ends.

They cut up the animals' flesh and hung it in the sun to dry on the end of a pole. Then they rolled it up tightly, and put it aside for the winter.

If they wanted to go on a journey by water, they paddled up or down stream in a canoe made of birch bark.

A favourite food was little cakes made of hominy or maize, for they grew corn, and stored it under the earth in baskets made of matting, instead of in a barn.

Once upon a time there was an American Indian hunter whose name was White Hawk. He was the handsomest, cleverest young man in the tribe: and, what's more, he knew just a little about magic, and whenever he liked he could turn himself into an animal. All the men in his tribe were very proud of him, but they did wish he would find himself a bride.

One day White Hawk wandered very far into the forest, and, quite suddenly, he found himself in a place which he had never seen before. It was not like the rest of the forest. It was a little clear grassy piece in the midst of the trees. It was round and very green, and quite open to the sky. Pink and white flowers were blooming in the grass, and at the edge there was a ring of brown earth.

White Hawk was very much astonished. He saw that no path led to this little garden, and he wondered how it came to be there. He thought to himself, "It must belong to *someone!* I'll hide at the edge of the forest, and perhaps in the cool of the evening someone will come and gather flowers in the garden." So he went to the edge of the forest and climbed up into a tree to keep watch.

31

He had not been there very long before the sky grew softly dark, the long shadows of the trees stretched across the ground like black candles, and stars grew out of the sky like flowers in a field. It was very still, for the birds had gone to sleep, and White Hawk could hear nothing but the croaking of the frogs. He was just thinking that perhaps he had better go home, when the faintest sound of music was wafted towards him. He slid along the branch of the tree and peeped through the leaves.

At first he saw nothing, but after a minute the music grew louder, and he became aware of a round black shadow in the sky. It came closer and closer, and as it drew nearer, it grew larger and more distinct and the music sounded like voices singing.

White Hawk gazed and gazed at the shadow. It was floating down, down, down, towards a pool of moonshine in the garden, and presently he saw that it was an enormous silver basket. "A basket floating down from the sky," thought White Hawk, "that's strange." But soon he became aware of something stranger still. The silver basket was not empty. It was full. Twelve beautiful girls were sitting in it, singing with voices as clear as water rippling over the pebbles in a brook.

White Hawk lay, without moving, on his branch, and said to himself, "Those aren't Indian girls. Those must be star maidens who live in the sky. How beautiful they are—more beautiful than the flowers in the forest."

The basket floated gently to the ground, and out stepped the star maidens, who began to dance. They swayed like corn in the wind and their long silky hair drifted behind them like wisps of cloud. And as White Hawk watched he saw that one of the star maidens was far more beautiful than the others. Her smile was as bright as a moonlight evening, her hair as dark as the forest at midnight, and her eyes were like two glimmering stars. Her voice was clearer, softer, sweeter than all the other voices. Her dancing was lighter than air, and the glitter of her feet was like dewdrops in the grass. White Hawk scarcely dared to breathe lest he should blow her away.

For a long while he lay silently watching. Presently, when it was very late, a cloud drifted in front of the moon, and the maidens, calling,

"Come! Come! Come!" sprang into the basket. As the music of the voices grew softer and softer, the basket floated up into the air—away, away, away until it disappeared among the stars.

White Hawk pulled his skin cloak closely round him, climbed down from the tree and walked home through the forest.

When he got home, he lay down on a buffalo robe and tried to sleep, but his head was so full of the mysterious star maidens in their silver basket that he never closed an eye. The next day he set out early

and he never stopped walking until he came to the lonely garden in the middle of the forest.

This time he did not hide. He said two magic words and changed himself into the stump of a tree overgrown with moss. That night when the moon was up there was a sound of music in the sky. Down floated the silver basket and out jumped the twelve star maidens. They began to dance, but soon one of them stopped. "Sisters," she said, and her face looked very frightened, "where did that come from?" She pointed to the tree stump into which White Hawk had turned himself. Then all the star maidens began to cry at once, "Come away, come away. It wasn't here before. Magic! It's magic!" Leaping into the silver basket, they floated up to the sky. White Hawk could hear their voices growing dimmer and dimmer, "Oh, magic, magic, magic!"

White Hawk changed himself back into a hunter and sat down to think. He was determined to see the star maidens again, and he wondered how he could manage to do this without frightening them. He looked about him thoughtfully, and presently, deep in the grass, almost·hidden from the eye, he spied the nest of a little field mouse. The mother mouse was there with her babies, and that put an idea

into White Hawk's mind. He whispered two magic words and turned himself into a field mouse and crept into the little nest.

The next night, when the star maidens came down to their garden, they found that the stump of the tree had disappeared and all was as usual. They leaped out of the basket and began to dance. The steps of their dance brought them nearer and nearer to the nest of the field mice, and at last the mice began to squeak "ee-ee," "ee-ee," "ee-ee," and run about in all directions.

How those star maidens laughed. "Come! Come! Come!" they cried, and ran in and out among the mice, chasing them. And the mice squeaked, "ee-ee," "ee-ee," and scattered about in all directions. Of course White Hawk was with them. He squeaked too, but he was rather clever. When the most beautiful of all the star maidens came near to him, he pretended to be frightened, and he cowered behind some long grass. With a laugh and a little cry of delight the star maiden stooped and stretched out her hands to pick him up. She saw the mouse shiver, and she heard two strange magic words. She felt herself caught by two strong arms, and when she looked up she saw the face of a young Indian hunter. "Sisters," she cried, "save me!" But it was too late. White Hawk carried her in his arms and ran and ran through the forest. The poor little star maiden saw the silver basket float up into the sky, and heard the sound of her sisters' voices growing fainter and fainter.

That's how White Hawk found his bride. He used to call her Starshine after they were married, because she had come down from the sky at night. They had a baby boy whom they called Half Moon, and if it had not been for that little boy, White Hawk might have lost his wife for ever.

This is how it happened:

One day the star maiden was lonely. She was very fond of White Hawk, but she used to get homesick. She longed to see the other star maidens, and one day when White Hawk was out hunting, she made herself a silver basket and she took Half Moon to the magic garden, and when she was in the middle of that little patch of green grass, she jumped into the basket with Half Moon in her arms. And the basket floated up into the sky.

Then a strange thing happened. When Starshine saw the other star maidens, she forgot all about White Hawk, and she stayed up in the sky and never thought about him once.

But it was different with Half Moon. He was growing into a fine little boy. He was not like the star people at all. He was just like a small Indian hunter. He used to wonder what had happened to the forests and the wild beasts, but most of all he wondered what had happened to White Hawk. He wanted his father badly, and one day he found the silver basket and floated down from the sky into the magic garden.

There, all by himself, sat White Hawk, looking very sad and lonely. When Half Moon saw him he jumped straight into his arms. White Hawk hugged him, and without really knowing what he was doing, stepped into the basket and floated up—up—up into the sky. There was Starshine with the other star maidens.

When Starshine saw White Hawk, she remembered him again and was glad to see him. After that they used to spend half the year in the sky and half the year in the forest, so they were all happy.

And when everyone is happy, it is time to end the story.

Tingletoo and the Shepherd Boy

(Scandinavian)

Today we would call the little people in Tingletoo and the
Shepherd Boy trolls but when this story was written they were
not so well known outside their native Scandinavia. Anyway
they are no doubt all related to the little people in other countries
—the leprechauns of Ireland, the piskies of Cornwall, the house-
brownies of Scotland and so on. Decidedly unreliable they all
seem, and inclined to unpleasant tricks at which they always
outplay any human audacious enough to challenge them. Never-
theless their antics make amusing reading!

This is a story about the little brown gnomes who used to live underground, among the roots of the trees, and in small hollow places
about which nobody knew.

They were dear little fellows, these brown gnomes, and always
very happy, unless they happened to lose something which belonged
to them. The worst thing which could happen to the underground
people was to lose their cap or their shoes. Even if they only mislaid
the little silver bell which hung on every cap, they were miserable;
for not a wink of sleep were they allowed to have until they found the
missing goods. That was a law in the land of the gnomes.

There was once a gnome who had the most musical little bell
imaginable. It rang so prettily and was so much more musical than any
of the other bells that he gave it a name. He called it "Tingletoo,"
and if you had been walking through the forest in the evening, when
the gnomes had come out, you would easily have found this particular
gnome because of the sweet sounds which came from Tingletoo.

Once, when the gnome had been dancing round a toadstool at the edge of the forest, the sun began to rise, and he slid underground as quickly as he could, for there are only four days in the year when the gnomes can appear in daylight, and even then they may not appear in their real form. They have to turn themselves into birds or beasts or even human beings. It was not the right time of the year for the little gnome to turn himself into something else, so he slid home as quickly as he could and went to bed, curled up under the root of a tree. But somehow he could not sleep.

He twisted and turned. He pulled some nice blanketty moss over his head. He tossed about. He got up and warmed a little mushroom soup in an acorn cup. But even that did no good. He was wide awake. He looked around. All the other gnomes were asleep and snoring, with the happiest expressions on their faces, and there he was—absolutely miserable. He could not sleep a wink.

"Tush! Tush! Tush!" said he crossly. "What in the world's the matter? This has never happened to me before. Here, Tingletoo, play me a tune!" And he called the words which he always used when he wanted Tingletoo to tinkle.

"Little bell
I love you well!
Tingletoo
Tinkle, do!"

But—there was no answer. In a flash the gnome knew what had happened. Tingletoo was lost. It must have fallen off his cap when he was dancing. The poor little gnome burst into tears. He knew that he would get no more sleep till the bell was found; besides, he loved Tingletoo.

Now the gnomes always go to bed in the day-time, and while this little one was trying to sleep, the sun had risen, and a shepherd boy came over the hills with his flocks.

First the shepherd boy looked up at the sky to see if it was going to be fine. Then he stopped at the edge of the forest and looked up at the trees and called to the birds. And when he had finished doing that, he sat down with his back against a tree trunk, and allowed his flock to wander about and nibble the green grass in the meadow which led to the wood.

As he sat there he saw a fine toadstool not far from the tree, and all around it glistened the dew. He dabbled his fingers in the dew. "Oh," said he, "how sweet and cool!" Just then he saw a drop which was larger and brighter than any of the others. He stretched out his hand and picked it up between finger and thumb, and found it was a tiny silver bell with a little thread hanging on to it. He tied it to one of his buttons, and whenever it moved it played so sweet a tune that the boy felt, somehow, happier than he had ever done before. And when the time came for him to seek work in another village, he took Tingletoo with him in his pocket and always felt happy.

Meanwhile, the poor little gnome was underground, and he could not get a wink of sleep. When night came and he could climb through the roots of the trees into the forest, he ran to the toadstool, but Tingletoo was not there. There was only the mark of a human hand. Night after night the little gnome hunted. Night after night he returned underground and went to bed sleepless.

At last a day came when he was allowed to appear in the world by daylight. Thinking that perhaps a magpie or a jackdaw had stolen Tingletoo he turned himself into a bird and searched every nest in the neighbourhood, but he could not find Tingletoo.

He sought high and low. He asked every bird, beast, fish and insect for news, but none of them knew anything about the lost bell.

At last the sun set, and the little gnome had to go back to his underground home and spend more sleepless nights until he could once again visit the world by daylight.

Time hung heavily on his hands, and he felt so terribly weary. He used to yawn, then run and lie down thinking that he could catch sleep unawares, but he couldn't; his eyes were wide open.

After long days and nights of weariness, there dawned another morning when he was allowed to visit the world by daylight.

Once again he turned himself into a bird, and this time he flew into the next village. There he came upon a number of sheep and near them their shepherd boy, sitting under a tree. Each of the sheep had a little bell round its neck, and as the gnome flew about disguised as a bird, he whispered,

"Say, do!
Have *you*
My bell;
O tell.
If so,
You know,
My sleep
You keep!"

But the sheep only said "Baa!" which perhaps meant "No," for the gnome was just going to fly away when the shepherd boy looked up and said, "What a strange bird, singing about a bell! Here, birdie, have you ever seen a bell like this?" and he pulled Tingletoo out of his pocket, and the air was filled with the merriest of chimes.

In a second the little gnome flew behind the nearest bush and turned himself from a bird to an old woman.

"Good day, my lad," said she to the shepherd, who rubbed his eyes, for he did not know where she had come from.

"That's a pretty bell you've got. How much will you take for it?"

"It's not for sale, mother," said the boy. "Ever since I've had that bell I've been happy. I wouldn't sell it for the world."

"The world's a big price, my son," said the old woman. "See! Here's a golden guinea."

"Gold is dross," said the boy. "It doesn't ring. My bell tinkles merrily wherever I go, so that my feet dance and my heart sings. The bell's not for sale, mother."

"Sit down by me," said the old woman. "I will tell you how to grow rich."

"I'd rather be happy, mother," said the boy, "but I'll listen if you like." So he sat down by the old woman and listened.

She began to tell him of all the secret charms of the underground folk, and how if they gave him a magic white stick, his sheep and his cattle would prosper and he would grow rich beyond his dreams. He knew that was true, for the underground folk never told lies. Then she told him of the wonderful world, the sea and the lands which lay beyond it, the great cities, the mines where the glittering jewels were hidden. "All that you can see," she said, "if your cattle make you rich beyond your dreams."

On and on she spoke, and the boy's eyes glittered and his heart beat fast. "Oh, if I had the white stick," said he, "I would give up my bell and be rich beyond any dreams!" Tears were in his eyes. "Oh, if only I had the white stick!" he said again.

"I have it here, my son," said the old woman.

Then the shepherd boy took the white stick and put Tingletoo into the old woman's hand.

There was a puff of wind, a wisp of cloud and the old woman floated away and disappeared in the air, and afar off, deep down in the earth, the shepherd boy seemed to hear a voice singing,

"Little bell
I love you well!
Tingletoo,
Tinkle, do!"

There came the thinnest echo of a sound, a tinkling music, which the shepherd boy had loved so well. He started up. He looked at the magic white stick which would bring him riches. Then he gave a low cry and he lay down with his face on his arms and wept for the lost happiness which he had sold for the world.

But deep, deep under the ground a little gnome was asleep with a smile on his face.

The Three Strange Partners

(Central European)

The bat is a wonderful little creature, although it is so ugly. Its large ears and thin dark wings are so sensitive that they can feel, without touching, any object to which they happen to come near. That is why the bat, whose sight is very bad, can fly in the dark through a thick forest without striking a single tree trunk or branch.

By day bats like to hang head downwards in some dark place, such as a cave, a hollow tree, a barn or a church tower. They fly by night, and dislike alighting on the ground because they find it difficult to crawl.

There are about 300 different sorts of bats in the world. We say that they belong to the Chiroptera family. Chiroptera comes from two Greek words and means "hand-winged", so if ever you see a bat at close quarters, look at its wings and you will find that the bones correspond, roughly, to the fingers of your hand, with a little hook at the top which represents the thumb.

Cormorants dive as often in real life as they did in the story, because they live upon fish and are always hungry. They have long beaks with a cruel little curve at the end, and they are good swimmers. They live together in flocks and build their nests on rocks. Most mother birds feed their young by putting food into the little ones' open beaks, but Mamma cormorant does not do this. She opens her own mouth very wide so that her baby can push his head inside it and pull out pieces of half-digested fish.

This is a story about a cormorant and a bat who made friends with a bramble, and the result of their strange partnership.

Once upon a time, a cormorant and a bat were thoroughly discontented. The trouble was that they wanted to grow rich and they really did not know how to set about it.

"It's all very well for me," said the cormorant, "I quite enjoy myself, standing about on the rocks, and flying when I feel inclined. But that won't get me any further. What am I going to do when I'm old? I shall want to retire and live comfortably."

"Yes," said the bat very solemnly. (Curiously enough, the bat always *was* solemn.) No doubt he had an old head on young shoulders, because he took life very seriously. If you had seen how that poor bat *worried,* you would have been really sorry for him. He quite agreed with the cormorant that both of them ought to be saving up for their old age, but how to do it he hadn't a notion.

And then, of all things, a nearby bramble came to the rescue. He

called out to the bat one morning. (Oh yes, in those days the bat came out in the morning—he had nothing to be ashamed of *then*.) The bramble called out to the bat, "Bless my thorns and berries! Why so serious, Mr. Bat? What's the matter this time?"

"This is no joking matter, bramble," said the bat. "The cormorant and I are very serious, very serious indeed. Ahem—hem." He coughed nervously.

"Well, you're still not telling me what has happened," said the bramble. "Here's the cormorant. I'll ask him. I say, cormorant, for goodness' sake tell me what's the matter. Here's Mr. Bat as solemn as a judge. It's enough to make my thorns blunt. What's up?"

"Up?" said the cormorant, "we're *down*—down in the depths of despair. We want to grow rich and save up for our old age—and we don't know how to do it."

"You don't mean to say you're

making a fuss about *that!*" said the bramble. "Why, bless my thorns and berries, *trade's* the thing! Everybody's getting rich by trade. You buy something for sixpence and you sell it for a shilling—and there you are."

"Bramble," said the bat solemnly, "that's true, but what shall *we* do?"

"Yes," said the cormorant, "what shall *we* do?"

"Oh, bless my thorns and berries," said the bramble. "How stupid you are. Upon my word, I've a good mind to scratch you. Now look here, we'll go into partnership. We'll buy a ship and we'll take a cargo of wool across the sea and sell it to the foreigners. My dear bat! My dear cormorant! In a couple of years our fortunes will be made. I can't think why we never thought of it before."

"Bramble," said the bat, "you are a most intelligent creature. You shall be senior partner."

"Bramble," said the cormorant, giving one of the berries a playful peck, "I'll go and order the boat at once. You go and collect the wool. There are some sheep over there."

Away flew the cormorant and bat to make arrangements with an old sailor who had a boat, and the bramble began to bargain with the sheep.

Anyone who knows anything about sheep, knows they are rather nervous, stupid creatures, and they never seem to know their own minds. They go first this way and then that, and then follow one another. They simply don't know how to be independent. And that is exactly what the sheep did when the bramble talked to them. The big ones said "Baa-ba" and the little ones said "Maa-ma," and then they all came up to the bramble in a bunch and just stared.

The bramble began to get annoyed. Its berries grew quite red and its voice scratchy.

"Don't you understand?" it asked. "I want wool to sell across the sea."

"Maa! Baa!" said the sheep, and at last the bramble gave it up in despair and asked the shepherd what to do.

"Wool?" asked the shepherd. "Why, my dear bramble, of course you shall have wool. The very next time I shear the sheep I'll remember

you and your partners. You shall pay me as soon as you get some money. Good day to you. I wish you a very prosperous future, I'm sure."

The sailor was just as kind about the boat as the shepherd had been about the wool. As neither the cormorant, the bat nor the bramble had any money, they agreed to pay for the wool and the boat after they had sold the first cargo.

At first everything went well. The cormorant was captain, the bat was a passenger, because he was going to do the selling, and the bramble was crew. All the wool was stacked on the ship, the sails were hoisted, and away went the three partners, tremendously excited about their new venture, and convinced that when once they had paid for the wool and the boat they would soon get rich.

And then a dreadful thing happened.

At first all was plain sailing and they thoroughly enjoyed the trip, but before they had got halfway they began to feel worried. The wind began to blow and the waves began to rock and the ship began to roll.

The poor bramble grew quite green and the bat hung upside down from a spar, feeling very peculiar indeed, and the Captain Cormorant couldn't get a stroke of work out of either of them. He had to fly up and down and do the odd jobs himself.

He encouraged them and tried to cheer them up. He scolded them and pecked them. He even went so far as to sneer at them, and call them "silly, feeble cowards". But it was of no use. The bat and the bramble were far too seasick to do anything, and all the time the waves were getting rougher and the winds wilder and the sky blacker. Thunder crashed and lightning flashed, and the little wooden ship was dashed hither and thither, while the water poured over the sides, and the three partners and their precious cargo of wool were soaked.

"Oh-h-h-h-h," groaned the bat, and "Ah-h-h-h," shivered the bramble, and "For goodness' sake stop grumbling and *do* something!" shouted the cormorant, doing his best to make himself heard above the wind. But the bat and the bramble continued to shiver and groan and the storm grew worse and worse.

At last the cormorant gave a loud screech. "Hi-bat, bramble, look out! Save yourselves."

The ship gave a terrible splitting sound, and, before the bat and the bramble knew what was happening, it broke in half and sank to the bottom of the sea.

It was a very lucky thing that the cormorant was there. Otherwise it is certain that the bat and the bramble would have been drowned, for the silly creatures were struggling together in the water, refusing to let go of one another, and the waves were washing them farther and farther away. "Oh dear, dear, dear," cried the cormorant. He flew after them, swooped down, seized the bramble in his beak, flew off again with the bat clinging to the bramble and the bramble swinging in the air.

Well, you can imagine that they were all nearly exhausted when they reached the shore. Exhausted and depressed.

They had lost the wool and the boat, and they had not paid for either.

"Oh dear!" groaned the bat, "we shall never again be able to show our faces, if we don't pay our debts."

"We'll have to get that boat back somehow!" said the cormorant; "I shall never stop looking till I find it."

"There's not much good finding it if the cargo's lost," grumbled the bramble. "Somehow or other, I'll have to get some more wool."

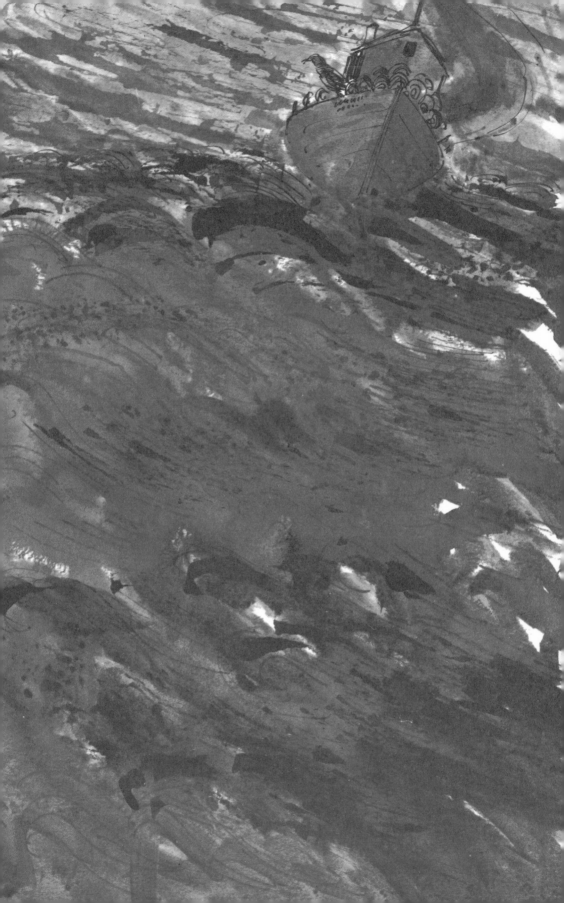

But, alas, they never replaced their loss. This is why the bat only comes out at night. He is afraid to show his face because he is still in debt.

And if you go down to the seashore, you will still see the cormorant diving for the boat. He dives and he dives, but he has never found it.

And as for the bramble; well, he is always catching on to the sheep, trying to collect more wool, and if you go too near, he will tear your clothes, because he has never been able to get enough stuff yet.

Lazy Carlos
and the Enchanted Fiddle

(Spanish)

Do you know what a fiddle is? Perhaps you call it a violin, which is a grander name. The great-great-grandfather of the violin is supposed to have come from the East. People say that there was once a king of Ceylon who lived five thousand years before Christ. He loved music, and he made himself a little box-like instrument with two strings stretched across it. On this he played strange wild music. To-day, if you meet a wandering minstrel in India, you will know that he is using the instrument invented so long ago by the King of Ceylon.

The Arabs used to play on a one-stringed fiddle, called a rebek. It was brought to Europe, and for hundreds of years people studied it, making instruments a little like it, but differently shaped and with more strings, until, about three hundred and fifty years ago, an Italian and his grandson made the perfect violin.

This Italian was called Andrea Amati, and his grandson was Nicolo. They lived in a little town near Venice, called Cremona, and taught other people to make such beautiful violins that Cremona became famous.

Antonio Stradivari, the man who is called king of violin makers, was first a pupil and then a master at the old school of Cremona. He made the body of his violins from a special pine which grew on the hills near the town, and he invented a beautiful amber-coloured varnish, the secret of which has been lost. He used to write his name on every instrument which he made. But when he grew older his sight began to fail, and then he would not sign because he was afraid that he might have left some flaw unnoticed.

The viola, the violoncello and the double-bass all belong to the same family as the violin. In the hands of a great musician there seems to be enchantment in the strings, but a lazy Carlos could never learn to play them, for a stringed instrument needs years of study, practice and patience.

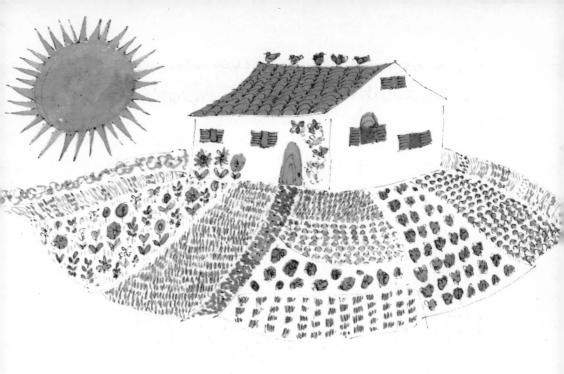

Once upon a time there was a Spanish boy whose name was Carlos. He lived with his grandmother in a neat little house at the top of a steep hill.

Carlos had a light heart and a merry smile, but he was so lazy that he had never been to the bottom of the hill, because he knew that if he did so, he would only have to climb up again.

His grandmother did her best to cure him of his idleness. At first she tried to coax him with kindness, but he only smiled lazily. Then she began to punish him, but he was still too lazy to mend his ways.

Do what she would, she could not make Carlos work. He was bone idle. He would not even earn a few pence to provide himself with clothes, and so he had nothing to wear but an old cloak, a torn shirt and a pair of ragged breeches which his grandmother had mended so often, and with so many different bits of stuff, that they looked like a patchwork quilt.

. One day, when Carlos was expecting his usual scolding, his grandmother came into the kitchen. Carlos opened his sleepy eyes and looked at her in surprise. Instead of crying, "Ah! You lazy, good-for-nothing boy," she sat down in a rocking chair, put a cushion behind her head and began to doze. "Good night Carlos," she said, "I've had supper," and she fell asleep without giving the boy anything to eat.

Carlos was too lazy to cook supper for himself, but he was hungry enough to be disappointed, and he almost felt that a scolding and a good supper would be better than no scolding and no supper. He was, however, so comfortable in the chimney corner that he yawned twice and did not give the matter another thought.

The next day his grandmother went out to work as usual, but instead of saying, "Ah! You lazy good-for-nothing, wait till I come back to-night and you'll be sorry if you don't go out and earn a few pence," she tied the last piece of bread and the only remaining onions in a handkerchief, and left the house without a word.

Carlos was too lazy to call after her, but when she came back in the evening, sat in the rocking-chair and dozed, saying, "I've had supper," he looked up slowly and said, "I'm hungry."

His grandmother only smiled. She opened one eye lazily. "What a pity," she said, and fell asleep.

Carlos tightened his belt and hoped for the best, but the next morning his grandmother went off without a word, and when she came back that night she said, "I've had supper," sat down in the rocking-chair and began to doze.

"I'm hungry," grumbled Carlos.

"I'm lazy," said his grandmother. "Too lazy to skin the onions, if I had any in the house, too lazy to cook the supper, Carlos, you bad boy. I've darned your cloak till there is more darn than cloak, and I am too lazy to darn it again. I've patched your breeches till there are more patches than breeches, and I am too lazy to patch again. *But I'm not too lazy* to send an idle good-for-nothing about his business. Be off, for not another meal will you get, not another stitch will I put in your clothes until you earn some money." With that she whisked off her slipper and seized Carlos by the collar.

The first whack that she gave him was so sudden that Carlos shot through the door with his grandmother after him, and the second whack was so hard that he flew over the garden gate with his grandmother clutching his cloak, and the third whack was followed by so many others that Carlos rolled from the top to the bottom of the hill without stopping. Of course, he was much too lazy to climb up again, which was perhaps rather a good thing, for his grandmother was still at the top, clutching her slipper and saying, "But I'm not too lazy to send an idle good-for-nothing about his business."

Carlos lay on his back in the dust, feeling very hungry inside and very battered outside, but far too lazy to move, so he curled up and went to sleep. He awoke next morning, feeling emptier than ever. While he was idly wondering what would happen next, a squeaky little voice suddenly broke in upon his thoughts, saying:

"Hullo, lazy Carlos! What are you doing?"

"Nothing," said Carlos.

"H'm," said the voice. "Nothing, as usual. But from what I have just seen, I rather think you'll have to begin to do something. You see, Carlos, you're far too lazy to climb up the hill and go home. And even if you did, the old lady's at the top to whip you down again, and, if I'm not mistaken, you're too lazy to ward off the blows. What are you going to do? You can't lie here in the dust forever!"

Carlos rolled slowly round in the direction of the voice.

"Don't know and don't care," he said, and opened one eye.

His astonishment made him not only open the other, but sit up slowly and hug his knees. In front of him was a little old man with a long beard and twinkling grey eyes. His cheeks were withered, but rosy. His hands and feet were long and thin. He was no higher than a three-legged stool, and in his arms he carried a fiddle which was as big as himself.

He shook his head severely at Carlos. "Aren't you hungry?" he asked.

"Umm," answered Carlos.

"Well, then," said the little old man, "hadn't you better earn a dinner?"

"Can't," said Carlos. "Never done any work! Don't know how." And he rolled over on his back again and grinned sleepily at his strange visitor.

The little old man looked at him cunningly.

"Listen, Carlos," said he, "I like that cloak of yours. I know it's darned and old, but it would make me a fine suit. As you see, I'm in rags. If I tell you how to earn a good meal without working for it, will you give me your cloak?"

"To be sure," said Carlos, "you can take it now if you like," and he sat up slowly and yawned while the old man unfastened the cloak, folded it neatly, and put it on the ground beside him.

"Now," said the little creature, "take this fiddle! Mark my words! The first tune that the fiddle plays will bring you a good dinner! The second tune that the fiddle plays will save you from prison, and the third tune will cure you of your idleness for the rest of your natural days."

With these words he vanished as suddenly as he had come, and Carlos was left on the road with the wind blowing through his ragged shirt, his cloak nowhere to be seen, and a small brown fiddle in his hand.

Putting the instrument idly under his chin, he drew the bow across the strings, and before he knew what was happening, the fiddle began to play the merriest dance that he had ever heard.

"Fiddle-dee-dee! Fiddle-dee-dee!
Fiddle a meal for Carlos and me!"

Faster and faster it jigged, now loudly and now softly.

Presently along the road came an old woman going to market. She carried a basket on each arm, and in one she had butter and in the other eggs. She was walking slowly, for her baskets were heavy, and every now and then she stopped and put them on the ground to rest her arms.

At first she did not hear the fiddle, but as she drew nearer, the merry tune wafted towards her on the wind, and she began to shuffle her feet and nod her head in time to the music, while the fiddle went on playing,

"Fiddle-dee-dee! Fiddle-dee-dee!
Fiddle a meal for Carlos and me!"

As she drew nearer, the old woman began to jig and to hop, jigetty-jig, hipetty-hop. The eggs in the basket hopped, too. Bump, bump! went the butter. Lazy Carlos still held the fiddle, and the fiddle played faster, louder,

"Fiddle-dee-dee! Fiddle-dee-dee!
Fiddle a meal for Carlos and me!"

On came the old woman, leaping in the air, curvetting and spinning like a top. The baskets bobbed and slipped, the eggs went hipetty-hop, and the butter went bumpetty-bump, and still the fiddle fiddled faster,

"Fiddle-dee-dee! Fiddle-dee-dee!
Fiddle a meal for Carlos and me!"

The old woman was now in front of Carlos, dancing wildly. The tears were pouring down her cheeks. Her hat blew away and her apron came undone. Her grey hair fell over her face, the soles flew off both her shoes, and she danced in her stockings, gasping for breath and screeching, "Stop it! Will you stop it?"

But when she screamed "Stop it!" the fiddle squeaked "Hop it," and fiddled faster than ever until the old woman seemed nothing but a wheel of whirling petticoats. Round and round she span on jigging feet. The baskets danced off her arms, and out of them hopped the eggs and the butter, jigetty-jig, bumpetty-bump, leaping and skipping on the road, until at the very feet of Carlos they crashed into one another. And when he looked down, there was nothing on the ground but an enormous omelette, wobbling to the tune of

"Fiddle-dee-dee! Fiddle-dee-dee!
I've fiddled a meal for Carlos and me!"

With a lazy laugh, Carlos put down the fiddle and stretched out his hand. He broke off a piece of the omelette and ate slowly. His grandmother had kept him without food for so long that each mouthful seemed to him more delicious than the one before.

Meanwhile, the old market-woman, exhausted after her dancing, had been sitting in the road, trying to recover her breath. At first she had been too giddy to watch what was happening, but when she had stopped trembling and could open her eyes, she saw the broken egg-shells in the road and the empty butter-basket.

"You thief!" she cried angrily. "You've stolen my butter and my eggs. You wicked, wicked boy. I'll tell the judges and I'll have you sent to prison!"

Carlos smiled sleepily and patted her shoulder. He had no idea that the fiddle would behave so oddly, and would have explained matters if he had not felt too lazy to take the trouble. Instead, he wiped his mouth with the back of his hand and offered the old woman the last bit of omelette. "I've never tasted such a good one," he said.

At this the old woman grew angrier than ever, and she began to shout so loudly that some farmers who were also on their way to market came up to ask what was the matter. Carlos rolled over on to his back and blinked at them, but the old woman burst into tears, and pointing at her empty baskets, cried, "While I stopped for a minute to dance to his fiddling, he robbed me of all my butter and eggs."

When the farmers heard this, they looked at the broken egg-shells and then at Carlos, and seeing a yellow streak of egg on the back of his hand and mouth, they fell upon him and began to push and drag him along the road, shouting, "To prison with the thief! To prison, to prison!"

Matters began to look very unpleasant for Carlos, but fortunately he remembered the words of the little old man, "The second tune that the fiddle plays will save you from prison"—and wriggling out of the farmers' hands, he managed to put the fiddle to his chin and draw

65

the bow across the strings. In an instant the fiddle had begun to play the merriest tune that can be imagined, and before the angry farmers knew what they were doing, they had begun to shuffle their feet and clap their hands in time to the music.

Carlos turned and began to walk back towards his grandmother's house, fiddling softly, while the farmers and the old market-woman came dancing behind him. Shuffle, slide, jig, hop, jig. They looked at their feet in a puzzled way, and then began to shout, "Stop it!" But when they screeched "Stop it!" the fiddle squeaked "Hop it!" and on they danced up the hill, while the fiddle played faster and faster.

"Fiddle-dee-dee. Fiddle-dee-dee.
There'll be no prison for Carlos and me."

The farmers' cloaks were flying in the wind. Their hats blew off and rolled down the hill. They kicked their legs and they waved their arms. They whirled and they twirled, imploring for mercy, but still the fiddle played faster and faster,

"Fiddle-dee-dee. Fiddle-dee-dee.
There'll be no prison for Carlos and me."

"Stop, stop!" they screamed, and "Hop, hop," answered the fiddle, until at last Carlos had pity on them and promised that if they would agree not to send him to prison, he would put down the fiddle.

Terrified lest they should be made to dance for the rest of their lives, the exhausted farmers promised, and when he had watched them dancing half-way down the hill again, Carlos tucked the fiddle under his arm and walked lazily into his grandmother's cottage.

The old lady was sitting by the fire eating a fried onion. When she saw her grandson come into the cottage as lazily as ever and prop an old brown fiddle in the chimney corner, she flew into a passion. "Ah, you lazy, good-for-nothing boy!" she cried. "So that's what you do when I send you out to earn a few pence. I'll teach you to spend your time fiddling silly dance tunes instead of working," and she seized the fiddle and was about to throw it into the fire when she thought that she would like to try it herself. She put it under her chin and scraped the strings with the bow. In the twinkling of an eye the fiddle was playing the liveliest tune imaginable.

"Fiddle-dee-dee. Fiddle-dee-dee.
Lazy Carlos shall dance for me."

Carlos looked down at his feet. In spite of himself, they were beating time to the music. He began to shake his head, lift his elbows and snap his fingers. The fiddle played faster.

"Fiddle-dee-dee. Fiddle-dee-dee.
Lazy Carlos shall dance for me."

Carlos jumped from his chair and began to jig round the kitchen table. "Stop it!" cried he, and "Hop it," answered the fiddle, playing louder and quicker as Carlos leaped and kicked.

"Fiddle-dee-dee. Fiddle-dee-dee.
Lazy Carlos shall dance for me."

Shuffle, jig, jump. Jump, jig, shuffle. Carlos was dancing madly now. He was panting for breath, but still the fiddle played and still he danced. He turned somersaults over the chairs. He leaped till he banged his head on the ceiling. He twirled round and round, hitting himself against the walls. He waved his arms and kicked his legs. Strips of his ragged shirt caught and tore. His shoes flew off and his garters burst. His braces fell over his heels and tripped him up, but he went on dancing. "Stop it. Stop it," he begged, and "Hop it, hop it," answered the fiddle, and played the faster.

"Fiddle-dee-dee. Fiddle-dee-dee.
Lazy Carlos shall dance for me."

Backwards, forwards, sideways, on his feet and on his head danced Carlos, imploring for mercy, panting for breath, but his grandmother took no notice. She still held the bow in her hand, the fiddle under her chin, and jigging and howling, Carlos tripped up and down the kitchen.

"Put it down, grandmother. Put it down!" he cried, but the old lady took no notice, and the fiddle played faster than ever.

"Fiddle-dee-dee. Fiddle-dee-dee.
Don't stop playing a tune on me
Till Carlos says that he'll work for thee."

Up and down danced Carlos, twirling and whirling, jigging and jogging, shouting, "Stop, I say! I'll work. I'll work. Boo-hoo, hoo-hoo. I'll WORK," until at last his grandmother took pity on him and put the fiddle and bow on the table.

Carlos lay blubbering in a heap on the floor. He was too exhausted to move, but he saw through his tears that his grandmother had picked up the fiddle and the bow, and was locking them in a big wooden chest where she kept her treasures. She carried the key on a string round her neck, and so never again was Carlos able to play on his fiddle.

Ever since that day he has been a hard worker, for if he gives the slightest hint of laziness, his grandmother has only to take out her key and walk over to the chest, whispering,

"Fiddle-dee-dee. Fiddle-dee-dee.
Lazy Carlos shall dance for me."

The Princess
who wouldn't Smile

(Danish)

This story should really be told more fully, as the Danes them-selves do. Each time a new person "sticks", repeat all the others, always ending "and Sammy solemnly trundled faster and faster". It makes the story so much better fun, but it is rather difficult to do it well, and you are almost certain to leave somebody out by mistake.

Once upon a time there was a man who had two sons. The elder was as solemn as a judge and the younger as perky as a sparrow, and so they were known as Solemn Sammy and Perky Peter.

Solemn Sammy and Perky Peter lived with their parents in a small village in Denmark, a few miles away from the King's palace. Every day they trudged along a narrow, rough road, carrying milk and eggs to the King's kitchen. And every morning they asked the King's cook the same question, Sammy solemnly and Peter perkily.

69

"Good morning cook, and how is Her Royal Highness the Princess Lili to-day?"

"Hallo, cook! What's the news this morning?"

And every day they would be given the same answer. "I am sorry to tell you, young men, that Her Highness has not given the ghost of a smile!"

Then Solemn Sammy would shake his head and say solemnly, "Dear, dear, dear!" and Perky Peter would shrug his shoulders and say perkily, "Well, well, well!" And back to the village the two brothers would go, Sammy solemnly and Peter perkily.

The trouble was that the King of Denmark's only daughter would not smile. Whether she wouldn't or whether she couldn't, nobody knew. They only knew that she didn't. That was all. The King used to scold her and the Queen used to coax her, but she still didn't even try to smile. They had story-tellers come to the palace to tell her the funniest stories in the world, but there wasn't so much as a twinkle in her eye. They had jesters to make jokes, but instead of laughing she

yawned. They had painters to make funny pictures and dancers to do comic dances, but she only stared at them with large, serious eyes and said, "How stupid they are!"

The King and Queen very soon became alarmed. They thought that their darling Lili must be ill, and they sent for the best doctors in the kingdom. One by one the doctors arrived with their little black bags and their long-tailed coats. Some were old and some were young and some were middle aged. Some were fat and some were thin and some neither one thing nor the other. Some were bald and some were hairy and some just betwixt and between, but none of them could make the princess smile. They felt her pulse and they tapped her chest and they listened to her heart. But she didn't smile. They gave her pills and tonics and cod-liver oil, but she only looked crosser than ever. They stood round her bed and looked at her mouth, saying, "Open—your Highness—a leetle wider—now smile." But the princess only put out her tongue, and the King, in a rage, sent all the doctors packing.

He turned to the princess. "Lili," said he, "come here."

The princess dropped a curtsy and looked frightened.

"Now," said the King, "smile. Do you hear me? Smile at once!"

Two large tears oozed out of the princess's eyes, rolled down her cheeks and dropped with a little splash on to the floor. But she didn't smile.

The King stamped his foot. His face began to get red and he looked like an angry turkey. He shook the princess by the shoulders. "*Now* will you smile? Do you hear? Smile! *Smile!* SMILE!" But the louder he shouted the lower did the corners of the princess's mouth droop, and a smile seemed farther away than ever.

"Very well, cry-baby," said the King, "I shan't ask you again, but the first man who makes you smile shall marry you and have half my kingdom into the bargain. So that's that!" And he left the princess to sulk by herself and went to arrange matters.

What commotion and noise! Heralds went dashing all over the country, blowing trumpets and shouting, "Oyez! Oyez! This is to give notice that the first man who makes the princess smile shall marry her and rule the half of Denmark. God save the King!" Naturally lords and commons, soldiers and sailors, tinkers and tailors and candlestick-makers came tearing up to the palace to try to make the princess smile. But she either looked cross or she looked bored or she began to cry, and all the unsuccessful suitors were tarred and feathered, until, at last, there was scarcely a barrel of tar or an ounce of feathers left in the country.

Now all this time Solemn Sammy and Perky Peter were bringing eggs as usual to the King's kitchen. Every morning Sammy said solemnly, "Good morning, cook. How is Her Royal Highness the

Princess Lili to-day?" And, every morning, Peter said perkily, "Hallo, cook! What's the news this morning?"

And every morning they would be given the same answer, "I am sorry to tell you, young men, that Her Highness hasn't given the ghost of a smile, and another gentleman has been tarred and feathered."

Then Solemn Sammy would shake his head and say solemnly, "Dear, dear, dear!" And Perky Peter would shrug his shoulders and say perkily, "Well, well, well!" And back to the village the two brothers would go, Sammy solemnly and Peter perkily.

One day Solemn Sammy said to his brother, "Peter, I'm going to the palace to make the princess laugh."

Perky Peter chuckled. "Learn how to do it *yourself* first," said he. But he was a kind fellow, and he patted his brother on the back. "Well, well, well," said he, "off you go!" and Solemn Sammy went off solemnly.

He hadn't gone very far before he met an old woman. "Heyday, Solemn Sammy," said she, "where are you off to, and will you give me the food in your basket?"

"I'm off to the palace to make the princess smile," said Solemn Sammy solemnly, "and as for the food in my basket, you can have it all if you want it." And he handed her the basket.

The old woman took it. "Sammy," said she, "you've got a stupid face, but a good heart, and that's the best thing in the world. If you want to make the princess laugh, take this wheelbarrow. There's a bird carved on the front. If anyone touches the barrow, the bird will squeak, 'Pip!' You must cry, 'Stop!' and that person will stick till you say, 'Let go.' Good-bye."

"Good-bye," said Sammy solemnly, and he took the barrow and trundled it along the road, and he went on trundling it solemnly, till he solemnly trundled it into the King's garden.

"Hi!" cried the head gardener. "Hey!" shouted the under gardener, and "Goodness gracious me! The impudence!" said the lord high chamberlain, who was picking roses. "Stop him!"

The head gardener seized the wheelbarrow. "Pip!" squeaked the bird, and "Stop!" said Sammy, and the head gardener stuck to the wheelbarrow, which Sammy went on trundling faster and faster. "Hi!" shouted the under gardener, and pulled the head gardener by the coat-tails. "Pip!" squeaked the bird. "Stop!" said Sammy.

And the under gardener stuck to the head gardener, and the head gardener stuck to the barrow, and Sammy solemnly trundled faster and faster.

"Here! What? How? What d'you mean by it?" shouted the lord high chamberlain, and whacked the under gardener with his stick.

"Pip!" squeaked the bird. "Stop!" said Sammy, and the lord high chamberlain stuck with his stick to the under gardener, and the under gardener stuck to the head gardener, and the head gardener stuck to the barrow, and Sammy solemnly trundled faster and faster.

He trundled past the kitchen, and the scullery maid stuck to the lord high chamberlain. He trundled past the church, and the sexton said, "Come away you naughty girl!" and seized the scullery maid by the apron strings. The bird said "Pip!" Sammy said "Stop!" and the sexton stuck to the scullery maid and the scullery maid to the lord high chamberlain, and the lord high chamberlain to the under gardener, and the under gardener to the head gardener, and the head gardener to the barrow, and Sammy solemnly trundled faster and faster. He trundled through the village, and an old lame donkey stuck to the sexton because it tried to eat a carrot which was sticking out of his pocket. A little boy seized the donkey by the tail, and the schoolmaster came after the little boy with a birch rod, and three geese came

"gobble-gobble" after the schoolmaster, and the blacksmith came after the geese with a pair of tongs, and they *all* stuck.

And then—yes, *then* came the King and Queen. The King shook the blacksmith by the collar. "Pip!" said the bird, and "Stop!" said Sammy. "Your Majesty! Your Majesty!" said the Queen, and caught him by the belt. "Pip!" said the bird, and "Stop!" cried Sammy. And the Queen stuck to the King, and the King to the blacksmith, and the blacksmith to the geese, and the geese to the schoolmaster, and the schoolmaster to the little boy, and the little boy to the donkey, and the donkey to the sexton, and the sexton to the scullery maid, and the scullery maid to the lord high chamberlain, and the lord high chamberlain to the under gardener, and the under gardener to the head gardener, and the head gardener to the barrow, and Sammy solemnly trundled faster and faster back to the palace.

Just as the King lost his crown and the Queen her slippers Princess Lili looked out of her window. At the first glance her eyes twinkled, at the second glance her lips twitched, and at the third glance she burst into a peal of laughter.

"Let go!" said Sammy, and immediately everyone fell down plump! Off limped the donkey. Away flew the geese. The lord high chamberlain looked nervously at the King. The scullery maid slunk off to the kitchen. The gardeners hid behind the trees, and the sexton, the blacksmith and the schoolmaster chased the little boy all the way home.

But Sammy solemnly went up to the princess and said, "You're my wife!"

So she married him, and he ruled half the kingdom, with Perky Peter as lord high chamberlain. After that the princess smiled so often that people called her "Laughing Lili". This was very necessary, for Sammy was so solemn that she simply had to do enough smiling for two!

And that's the end of the story.

The Cotton Fairy

(Southern United States)

When this story was told slaves were employed on the cotton plantations. They not only looked after the cotton plants while they were growing but had to gather the "bolls", as the seed capsules are called, when they ripened and pick out the seeds from the cotton by hand before Eli Whitney invented his "gin" to do it mechanically. Now, too, the seeds are used for foodstuffs and other parts of the plants help in making many things from paper to explosives and cinema film to soap.

Once upon a time there lived a little lady on the edge of a swamp. She was a tiny little thing, so tiny that you could not have seen her if you had passed her in the street. She was just about as big as an acorn, so probably was a fairy. A person of that size couldn't be anything else. She was a most sweet little creature, and clever, too. She used to sit outside her tiny house and spin all day long. And how she could make her spinning wheel whir! She had made it from the wing of a fly, and it used to whirl round ever so quickly, making the little whirring sound that a fly makes when it gets excited. And the spindle on which she wound her thread was so small that one could scarcely see it. As a matter of fact, her friend the bee had given her his sting. And a very fine spindle it made.

At all hours of the day the fairy sat at her spinning wheel, and other fairies used to come and buy thread from her for their ball dresses. King Winter employed her to make the glittering silver wires with which he tied icicles to the trees. The flowers gave her work. They often wanted wee hairs on their leaves or their stems, and delicate tissues for their petals. She was a most useful little lady, *but somebody was jealous of her*.

It was the spider. Like the fairy, he was a very clever spinner. He used to make the most beautiful webs, all delicate like lace. He could spin very quickly, and run in and out among his own threads, but he never could make anything quite so fine as the fairy did, and he was jealous of her.

At last he made up his mind to drive her away from her home near the swamp; so he packed up his things and came to live next door to her. One morning when she woke up, she saw a shadow in front of her little house. She popped her head out of the window, and there, right across her front garden, was a web, and inside the web an enormous spider. He had great big glaring eyes and horrible legs covered with hairs. The poor little fairy grew pale with terror. She pulled down the window and drew the blind and then began to fan herself. She felt so faint that she drank up a whole dewdrop before she could make up her mind what to do.

At last she plucked up her courage and peeped through the keyhole. "Aha! *I* see you," said the spider. "Ee!" squeaked the fairy, all in a flutter. Her wings trembled so that she couldn't even fly for another dewdrop. She went to the window with her little breast heaving and her tiny little hands trembling. There she sat until the evening and then, when the shadows were long and the sky was pink, she lifted up the corner of the blind and the spider wasn't there.

As everyone knows, fairies are very changeable creatures, and this one was no exception. When she found that the spider had gone, she fluttered round the room, clapping her hands and laughing to herself with a sound so soft that it was like a harebell ringing. Then she picked up her spinning wheel and carried it out to the front doorstep, and began to spin and spin and spin, to make up for lost time. She was so happy now that the spider had gone that she started to sing.

Now, this was a silly thing to do, for the spider wasn't very far off, and it attracted his attention.

"Bo!" said he, as he bounced out. "Ee!" squeaked the fairy, and she seized her spinning wheel and ran with the great big hairy spider after her. He had so many legs that he could go pretty fast, but she had wings, and they helped, only unfortunately, when a fairy's frightened,

her wings aren't very much use. They go limp, and with limp wings you can flap a little, but you can't really fly, and, besides, the poor little fairy was carrying her spinning wheel, and so the spider gained on her.

He did his best to frighten her, too. He made his eyes all bulgy and made the hairs stick out all over his legs. "Bo! Bo! Bo!" he growled, and "Ee! Ee! Ee!" squeaked the fairy, still grasping her spinning wheel.

She fluttered and ran, fluttered and ran, fluttered and ran, till she stumbled and nearly fell into a mouse's hole. There was a little door in front of the hole, and it was shut. The fairy tapped. "Let me in, mousie, let me in! The spider's after me!"

The mouse came to the door, yawning. "What are you doing here at this time of night?" he said. "Go home at once!" "Let me in! Let me in!" cried the poor little fairy. But the mouse slammed the door in her face, and away she went, fluttering and crying.

"*I* see you," cried the voice of the spider, and "Ee!" squeaked the fairy, and ran faster. She was losing her way now, and she was very unhappy about it. Presently she saw a big face looking at her, and she recognised a toad. "Oh, Toad darling! Take me into your hole, just for one night." But the toad wasn't a gentleman. In fact he was rather a vulgar creature. He put out his tongue. That's all. He didn't speak a word, and gave no help, and the poor little fairy ran on.

It was getting so dark, and she knew the spider would soon catch up. "Where shall I go?" she cried. "Oh dear, oh dear, I can't see."

"Why, what's the matter, fairy?" asked a sweet little voice.

"I can't stop, I-I-I can't st-stop," stammered the fairy. "I want somewhere to hide. He's after me—he's going to catch me—Ee! Ee! Ee! he's coming!"

"There, there, there!" said the voice. "I'll hide you. Follow my lantern."

The fairy looked up and saw a tiny glimmering light in front of her, and she knew that she had found a friend. It was a firefly, and, of course, every firefly carries a tiny little lantern. The poor fairy was so exhausted that she could only take little fluttering steps.

"This way! Quick!" said the firefly, and he held his lantern low so that the fairy could see where she was going. She was growing terribly frightened because the spider was now so close that she could hear it breathing, and, of course, he could see the firefly's lantern, too, and as it was just in front of the fairy, he could see *her* much better than if she had been in the dark.

"Ho, ho, ho!" he said with a nasty spidery chuckle, "I see you. You wretched little spinner! Wait till I catch you in my web, I'll gobble you up, spinning wheel and all. Ha! I'm coming," and he made a sudden dash and got so near to the fairy that if the firefly hadn't suddenly pushed the lantern into his face and dazzled him he would have caught her.

"This way, this way!" whispered the firefly. He flew up into the air and the fairy followed, and found herself by a tall plant covered with pink flowers.

"Oh, oh, oh!" she cried, "he's coming!"

"Quick, get in there!" cried the firefly, and with a little gasp the fairy jumped into one of the pink blossoms.

"Aha!" snarled the spider, "I've got you, madam," and he stretched out a long hairy arm to snatch the fairy from her hiding-place.

There was a little sputter of laughter from the firefly.

"No luck," said he, for one by one the petals of the pink flower had closed, and there was the fairy, spinning wheel and all, safe and sound inside the bud. She nestled there quietly, and when she had quite got over her fright, she began to spin.

Now the spider was really furious. He rampaged up and down in

front of the flower, waiting for the petals to open. Then he settled on
the bud, and wove a web all round it, so that he could catch the fairy
when she popped her head out for a breath of fresh air.

But the fairy was wise. She stayed where she was. She had more room now, for she had discovered a little round place at the back of the flower, a pod, which was growing bigger. She used to hear the spider crawling about all round, but she knew he couldn't get her and she wasn't at all afraid.

"Come out, you wretched little spinster!" shouted the spider.

"Shan't," the fairy said, laughing gaily.

At last the spider was so angry that he flew into a rage, and trying to bite the pod where the fairy was hidden he missed and bit himself! And he gave himself such a fright that he went off in a temper and was never heard of again. So that was the end of *him*.

No sooner had he done this than the pod opened and out popped the fairy, spreading out all the lovely fluffy thread which she had spun while she was hiding. It hung like a fine white fluffy tassel from the pod, and it was the most beautiful work that the fairy had ever done.

People say that when the other fairies saw it they wanted to be spinners too, and they all took to living in the pink flowers of the cotton shrub. And that is why, at a certain season in the year when the pods are ripe, there are white fluffy tassels all over the cotton shrub.

From these white fluffy tassels men make thread. So you see what a useful little lady the fairy was. Lucky that the spider never caught her!

Gopala
and the Cowherd

(Indian)

In India, as in many other countries, especially in Asia, there are still many, many people who do not have sufficient to eat but who are prepared to go even hungrier to scrape together enough money to send their sons to school, they value learning so highly.

Once upon a time a poor widow lived with her little son on the edge of a forest in Northern India. The little boy's name was Gopala, and his mother loved him very dearly. She taught him to be good and truthful, and to say his prayers every night. Gopala, like many people in India, believed that there was more than one god, and the god to whom he always prayed was called Krishna.

Gopala's mother was very poor and rather ignorant, and she did not know how to read or write, so she could not teach her little boy his letters. When Gopala was five years old, his mother felt very much troubled. She said to herself, "He knows how to be good, but he must also know how to learn. I shall have to send him to school." Then she sighed and looked very sad. She was so poor, and she knew that before Gopala could go to school he would have to have neat clothes and a pen and an inkstand, and all sorts of things which would cost money.

However, she worked very hard at her spindle, and by the time Gopala was six years old she had spun so much cotton that she was able to sell it and buy the boy all that he needed. When the time came for him to go to school, she dressed him in his new clothes, put his pen and his inkstand in his hand, and sent him off to the teacher. Then she went back to her spinning and prayed to the god Krishna to look after her little boy.

Off went Gopala to school, but the road which led there was more than a mile long, and it passed through the forest. Gopala knew that there were fierce wild animals lurking behind the trees, and he felt a little bit lonely, but he ran as fast as he could. At school he soon

forgot his fear; he was so happy
that he played with the other boys
until they went home for supper.

Their homes were quite near to
the school. They did not know
when they sat by their mothers,
eating bowls of rice, that poor
little Gopala was running all alone
through a gloomy forest.

The sun was setting and it grew
darker and darker. The wild beasts

began to roar, and Gopala ran faster and faster, until, at last, he reached the edge of the forest and fell down at his mother's feet crying, "I'm frightened! I'm frightened! I can't go to school tomorrow."

His mother took him on her knee and comforted him. Then she made him some little cakes of rice, gave him a long drink of milk and put him to bed on a mat on the floor. She thought: "When he wakes up he'll forget all about it, and he'll go off to school quite happily." Then she went to bed herself, and she whispered a prayer: "O Krishna, take care of my little boy!"

The next morning Gopala awoke, but he had not forgotten the dark lonely forest and the wild beasts, and when it was time to go to

school again he cried: "Oh, I'm frightened! I'm frightened! I don't want to go to school again."

But his mother took his hands and walked with him to the edge of the forest. She said, "You mustn't cry. Just think to yourself, 'I've got a big brother in the forest who looks after some cows,' and then if you're frightened call out, 'Brother Cowherd, come and take care of me!'"

When his mother said this, Gopala began to feel brave again. He thought: "What fun to have a brother who keeps cows in the forest!" So he waved his hand and went off by himself while his mother prayed: "O Krishna, take care of my little boy."

Gopala went hopping and skipping along quite happily just at first, but soon the trees seemed to be very thick, and once or twice he heard a rustle among the leaves and he began to be a little frightened. His lower lip began to tremble, and he felt his eyes getting hot at the back, as though he were going to cry. He stood still and looked around. There was nobody there, and at last he cried: "O big brother, who looks after the cows, come and take care of me."

Then something happened.

There was a queer little whispering, rustling sound in the bushes, and from behind a shrub peeped a boy—a big boy with a beautiful shining smile. He had a golden crown on his head, and in the crown there was a long peacock's feather. He was a good deal bigger than Gopala, but he was very gentle. He went up to the little boy and said, "Come along, I'll take you to school, and when you come back I'll take you home again."

So little Gopala went along with the strange boy, and he felt quite happy and safe. When he reached the edge of the wood the stranger disappeared, and Gopala ran into school.

That evening when he started to go home through the dark, gloomy forest he did not feel at all frightened. He just called out: "O big brother, who looks after the cows, come and take care of me," and again, from behind the bushes, came the beautiful boy with the golden crown.

After that Gopala went to school quite happily every day. Every

morning his mother took him to the edge of the wood and prayed:
"O Krishna, look after my little boy"; and every night Gopala came
back safe and happy, saying: "I do love my big brother who keeps
the cows."

One morning, after Gopala had been going to school for nearly a
year, the teacher said, "I am going to have a feast at my house next
week, and I want all my little pupils to come too."

The boys were very excited. They did not have a feast very often,
and, of course, they made all sorts of plans, and the best plan of all
was that each one should bring the teacher a present.

"I shall bring sweets," said one.

"And I shall bring a little cake made of rice," said another.

"And I shall bring a curried chicken," said another.

Then they all ran home as quickly as they could to ask their mothers
to prepare presents for the feast. Gopala, too, thought, "I must give
something." But when he reached home he found that his poor
mother had no money and no food in the house except a few grains
of rice. She could not give Gopala any supper or any breakfast, so,

of course, she could not give him a present for the feast. Gopala was very sad, and that night, when she put him to bed on his little mat, his mother prayed, "O Krishna, comfort my little boy."

The next day poor Gopala went slowly through the forest. He was very hungry and he had nothing to give the teacher. He did not want to be different from the other boys, and he knew that they were all bringing presents for the feast.

At first he did not know what to do, and he very nearly cried. Then suddenly he remembered, "Why! I'll ask my big brother."

So he stood quite still and called out, "O big brother, who looks after the cows, come and take care of me." And out of the bushes came the boy with the golden crown and the peacock's feather.

At once Gopala told him his trouble, and the beautiful stranger smiled, then he went back into the bushes and returned with a little bowl of curds. "Give this to your teacher, Gopala," he said, and disappeared.

Carefully holding the bowl between his hands, Gopala went joyfully to school, and there he found everybody giving presents to the teacher. There were cakes and sweets and curry and fruit, but nobody had brought a bowl of curds.

The teacher was pleased. He took the bowl and he poured the curds into a jar.

Then a strange thing happened.

When he was giving the bowl back to Gopala he found that it was quite full, as though he had never emptied the curds into the jar. He was very much astonished. Once again he poured out the curds into a jar, and once again he looked at the bowl and it was still quite full. He did this over and over again until the whole school had a dinner of curds, and yet the little bowl was still full.

The teacher looked at Gopala. "Gopala!" he said, "Where did you get this present?"

"Oh," said Gopala, "I got it in the forest. My big brother, who looks after the cows, gave it to me."

Then the teacher said, "I want to see your big brother." Little Gopala led his teacher into the forest. As usual, he stood quite still and called: "O big brother, who looks after the cows, come and take care of me and my teacher!"

As usual there was a rustling and whispering among the bushes, but no beautiful stranger came to Gopala.

Gopala called again, "O big brother, who looks after the cows, come and take care of me and my teacher!" But the boy did not come; only a voice like a silver bell answered "A long time will pass before your teacher may see me. But you, Gopala, are blessed, for very few boys have a mother like yours."

Of course, what had happened, was that every day Gopala's mother had prayed: "O Krishna, take care of my little boy!" and Krishna had heard the prayer and pretended to be the big brother who looked after the cows.

The Shepherd's Treasure

(Persian)

The people of Persia, like those of other Eastern lands, have many proverbs and wise sayings which have been passed from father to son, so that they have never been forgotten.

Here are some which the shepherd in the story which follows may have known.

1. The sheep were not made for the shepherd, but the shepherd for the service of the sheep.

2. He that plants thorns shall not gather roses.

3. Patience is a tree whose root is bitter, but its fruit is very sweet.

4. To be a friend of the foolish is like kissing a bear.

5. Soap will not make a black cat white.

6. Look upon him who is above thee as thy father; him who is thine equal as thy brother; and him who is below thee as thy son.

7. One pound of learning requires ten of common sense to get it.

8. To the thirsty a thousand pearls are not worth a drop of water.

9. A closed fist is the lock of heaven: an open hand is the key of mercy.

10. Time is the best teacher.

Once upon a time there was a poor man who herded sheep in Persia. His home was a cave in the hillside. His guardian was the old shepherd's staff which he carried when he brought his sheep from their grazing ground; and his best friend was the sheepskin which he wore over his tattered clothes by day, and wrapped round his body when he slept at night.

The shepherd had never learned to read or to write, and yet he was far wiser than many a teacher, for he knew the ways of every beast which prowled over the hills and through the forest. He learned the habits of every little insect which crept among the leaves and grass. He listened to the birds, and their songs taught him the joy of life. He watched the sky and the clouds, and learned from the wind when the rare, welcome rain would fall. Nature was his book; and in the ways of nature he was wiser than any man in Persia.

Every day, when he led his flock to the grazing ground, he met other shepherds, and because he made friends with them and talked to them, he grew to understand the ways and thoughts of his fellow men.

As time passed, the people who lived in the towns heard about the shepherd and came to see him when they were in trouble. "You are wise," they would say. "Help us in our difficulty." Then they would tell their stories. Sometimes they were unhappy because they had quarrelled with their neighbours. Sometimes they were troubled because they had once been rich but now were poor. Sometimes they were discontented, although they had once been poor and now were rich.

The shepherd listened to each one in turn, and because he loved his fellow creatures and had thought much about men and their troubles, he was able to give a wise answer, and the people who had come to

consult him went back to their homes comforted. Because the shepherd had helped them, they told their friends about him, and, little by little, his fame spread until it came to the ears of the Shah.

The Shah was a good king who was always anxious to do the best for his people and to find wise governors for the different parts of his kingdom. When he heard of the shepherd, he made up his mind to visit him secretly and discover whether he was as wise as people said.

One night he sent for his favourite servant. "Mustapha," said he, "I am about to make a long journey alone. No one must know me. Therefore, take away my silk clothes and my jewels and give me the oldest of your robes, and nothing but a grey cloak to cover them."

The servant did as he was told without asking any questions. He knew his master often disguised himself and wandered about the city,

mixing freely with his subjects so as to find out whether they were contented or unhappy. He was, however, a little astonished when the Shah asked for some bread and dates, saying that he was going to travel far from the city, and that he would be away for several days.

Wrapped up in an old cloak and carrying his food in a little bag, the Shah mounted a mule and rode out of the city gates across the sandy track to the hills.

As he jogged along, talking now and then to his mule and sometimes nibbling a date, his eyes gazed into the distance, but he saw nothing but the tufts of grass, the sand and a few low shrubs. He was beginning to wonder where he would find the shepherd when he saw in the distance what seemed to be a cloud of dust.

"Ah," said the Shah, "this must be a caravan of merchants journeying to the city. I will ask them whether they have seen the famous shepherd."

He pricked up his mule and rode towards the cloud of dust, but as he drew near he saw that it was not a caravan of merchants but a flock of sheep grazing on the hillside. The creatures had so little fear that they scarcely moved when he rode amongst them, and the Shah smiled, thinking to himself: "Aha, they have a good master."

"And where is your master, my friends?" he asked, drawing in his rein.

A man who was sitting at the entrance of a cave stood up and came towards him.

"Peace be with you, sir," he said. "May I offer you some goat's cheese to eat with your bread and dates? I have no wine, but the water in my bottle is fresh." He unhooked a skin bottle which hung at his waist, took off his tattered sheepskin and spread it on the ground with as much care as he would have done with an embroidered silken cloak.

"Rest," said he to the Shah, "for I see by the dust on your clothes and on your mule's coat that you have come from a long distance."

The Shah sat on the sheepskin and began to talk to the shepherd, asking him questions and listening carefully to his answers. He was amazed at the wisdom of each reply and the simple dignity of the

man's words. After a while he rose from his place and smiled at the shepherd, saying: "I thank you for your kindness, but I must now ride on, for I am only a poor traveller who has a long way to go."

The shepherd bowed low. "Sire," he said, "you are no poor traveller. You wear your tattered garments like a king. Your speech is the speech of a man who is accustomed to being obeyed. Your eyes are thoughtful and straight, the eyes of a man who commands. Your manner is courteous, the manner of one who meets many men, and must give due attention to each, whether he be great or small. Surely you are a king. Is not your servant, the shepherd, speaking to his Shah?"

When the Shah heard this, he took the shepherd by the hand and said, "The Shah is speaking to the wisest of his subjects, whom he will make governor of every village through which these sheep have passed."

From that time onwards, the shepherd ceased to keep sheep on the hillside. He became governor of the villages through which his sheep had passed. He lived in a little white house with a garden. Servants waited on him. He wore fine clothes. There were horses in his stable, and mules and camels to carry his luggage when he was travelling from place to place.

At first people in the villages were glad that he had been made their governor, for they had loved and trusted him for many years. But after a while, although he always gave them wise answers and kind advice, they began to distrust him. Wherever he went, he carried on the back of a camel a strong chest bound with iron and fastened with a double lock. The people began to whisper about this chest.

"Why does he guard it so carefully?" asked one. "Is there treasure inside it?"

"Perhaps," said another, "he keeps the money which we pay for our lands and our houses in that chest."

"That is not honest," said a third. "The money which we pay for our lands and our houses belongs to the Shah. Does our governor keep it for himself?"

Little by little they began to grow more suspicious, and before long everyone in the village was talking about the man who had once been an honest shepherd and now had become a dishonest governor.

"He robs the poor," muttered the women. "He steals the Shah's treasure," said the men. Even the children turned against him, saying, "He is afraid that someone will open the chest. That's why he guards it so carefully and has a double lock."

There is a proverb which says "Bad news travels quickly." After a while the story of the dishonest governor reached the palace. The Shah could scarcely believe his ears, but tale after tale was told him until he began to think that anything which had been stolen, anything which anyone had lost, was locked up in the dishonest governor's chest.

Disappointed and angry, he sent for his favourite servant. "Mustapha," he said, "bring me my grandest robes. Send for my best horses and my slaves. I go forth in state to make a journey."

The servant obeyed and within a few hours the Shah, followed by the greatest judges in the city, his most trusted nobles and a band of slaves, rode across the hills towards the governor's white house.

They had not been travelling for many hours before the Shah once again saw in the distance a cloud of dust. A shadow passed over his face and a look of sadness came into his eyes. He remembered that other journey when a cloud of dust had become a flock of sheep with a shepherd sitting at the mouth of a cave.

This time the cloud was larger, and, as the Shah drew nearer, he saw that it was the governor and his servants riding out to meet him.

The governor was on a white horse, but behind him was a camel loaded with a wooden chest. The chest had a double lock and bands of iron. It was guarded by armed men, and the camel driver, who was leading the great beast by a scarlet rope, carried a spear.

When the governor came up to the Shah, he bowed to the ground. But the Shah only looked at him sternly. "What are these stories that

I have heard about you, O robber of the poor?" he asked, and one after another he repeated the tales which he had heard.

The governor shook his head. "I have stolen nothing. I have hidden nothing," he said.

"Then," said the Shah angrily, "open your treasure chest, and show me what is inside it."

The governor went up to the camel, touched it, giving a slight word of command so that it knelt on the ground. Then he took a key from a silk cord at his waist, stooped and opened the chest.

Nobles and judges leaned forward. Even the slaves stepped from their places. Only the Shah remained motionless, for the governor did not bring jewels and treasure from the chest. Out of it he drew a tattered sheepskin. He showed it to the Shah, and slowly began to take off the beautiful clothes which he was wearing.

"Sire," he said, "this, my best friend, is my treasure. I have kept it, carefully guarded, to remind me of the days when I wandered over the hills as a poor shepherd. I feared that good fortune might make me forget that once I had nothing but a sheepskin. I feared that I might forget to be humble. I have kept my old friend lest a time should come when my master would turn me once again into the cold world."

When the Shah heard these words, tears came into his eyes. He took his faithful servant by the hand and kissed him.

"O wisest of my subjects," he said, "from this time onwards you shall be the greatest of my governors."

And so the governor who had once been a shepherd became the most important man in the kingdom. But he never forgot to be humble, and to the day of his death he kept the old sheepskin which had been his best friend.

The Mannikins
and the Green Peas

(German)

Fairy stories are great travellers. Somebody once told them in one country. They were carried to another, another and another until gradually they moved nearly all round the world, changing slightly as they went. See if you do not think this story comes again, with a different setting later in this book.

Once upon a time there was a German village which always seemed to have good luck. The people who lived in it always looked rosy and well-fed. They had nice clothes to wear, enough to eat and to drink, just enough money in their purses to make them feel contented, and plenty of wood to burn on their fires when it was cold. The farmer had cows in the barn and sheep in the fields. The baker had plenty of good flour to make cakes and loaves. The schoolmaster had plenty of little boys and girls to teach, and when they were good, they were as good as gold, and when they were bad, they weren't *too* bad; they were just full of fun, that's all! There was enough milk for the cats, and there were enough bones for the dogs, and there was quite enough happiness to go round, which was surely the most important thing of all.

People from other places sometimes went to see that village, to try to find out what it *was* that made everybody so contented. But they couldn't see anything, and when they asked the villagers, the answer was always the same. "Ah! The mannikins live here." "But what are they like?" asked the other people. Always the same answer came. "We don't know! We've never seen them." And the strangers went away very much puzzled. But this is what they were like: they were tiny little men, no bigger than forks. They dressed in green—green caps, green jackets, green leggings and little green boots with long, pointed toes. Wherever they were, they brought good luck, for they were fairies.

They didn't live outside in the woods and the trees. They lived in peoples' houses. Yet nobody ever saw them, for they used to go to sleep in the day-time—hidden away somewhere—up in the chimney, curled up at the back of the plates on the dresser, behind the coal-scuttle, in the wood shed, in any place where they knew they wouldn't be disturbed. And then, when all the people in the house had gone upstairs to bed, and were snugly tucked up and fast asleep, out came the little green mannikins from their hiding-places, and played about like a lot of jolly children.

They had fun. They simply squeaked with laughter, and they didn't care what they did. They filled the sink with water and took baths. They turned the blind-cord into swings. They put butter all up the legs of the kitchen-table, then tried to climb up and, of course, slithered about all over the place. They rode on the cat's back round the room, and when pussy jumped, they all fell off in a heap with their legs in the air. They put the bread knife across the milk jug, and made it into a see-saw. They played ball with the lumps of sugar, and turned the plates into hoops. In fact, they had a splendid time, just like a party.

But they were good little fellows, these mannikins. They didn't play about in people's houses and do nothing in return. And they were very honest. If they had had a good time, they were willing to pay for it. At twelve o'clock at night, all the fun stopped, and the mannikins began to pay for their good time. And they did this by work. They simply rolled up their little green sleeves and began to do the work

of the house. Anyone listening at the keyhole would have heard them buzzing about like bees—and how they chattered!

"Brush the floor, brothers, take away the dust.
Polish all that ought to shine! Rub away the rust.
Wash each plate and dish and cup,
The mess you've made you must clear up!
Patch the clothes, brothers, don't you leave a hole,
Scour the sink, chop the wood! Go and fetch the coal.
Lay the table, black the shoes,
Clean the grate and brush the flues!
Do the work, brothers, get the whole thing done!
The mannikins say 'Thank you,' now they've had their fun!"

That's why the villagers always looked happy and contented. They left the mannikins in peace, and so the mannikins helped them. In fact they even made butter for the dairy-maid and bread for the baker. But the person whom they loved most of all was the tailor. They were *very* fond of him. Every night, before he went up to bed, he put out sugar and biscuits and any tasty little morsel which he thought the mannikins would like, and of course they were grateful, and at night they did half his sewing for him, and at last he grew so rich that he was able to marry.

But, unfortunately, he didn't choose his wife very wisely. It was a great pity that he didn't choose a wife from his own village. Instead, he went outside to a town quite far away, and he brought back a fashionable lady. She didn't wear wool or cotton. She wore silk and satin. She didn't wear her hair in two nice fat plaits like the village girls. She had it all curled and frizzled by the barber. She didn't wash her face in cold water till her cheeks glowed. *She* used warm milk to keep her skin white. She didn't cook the dinner and make the beds, but she had a little rosy-cheeked servant girl who came and did it for her. But the worst of it all was, she had heard of the mannikins and wanted to see them for herself! She used to look up the chimney and in the roof, and was always trying to find them, and at last her husband grew quite cross with her for being so inquisitive.

"You know quite well," he said, "that if once we set eyes on the mannikins they'll go away from the village and nobody will ever be lucky again."

"B-but I *w-want* to see them!" wept the spoilt little wife.

"Then want must be your master," said the tailor.

"I *will* see them!" said the wife, and stamped her foot. "I'll sit up all night and peep through the keyhole."

"That you won't!" said the tailor, and at bedtime he picked her up and carried her upstairs and locked the door.

The next day he thought she had forgotten all about it because she said nothing. He really thought she had turned over a new leaf, because she spent all day shelling peas in the kitchen. And when she went upstairs to bed she never said a word about the mannikins.

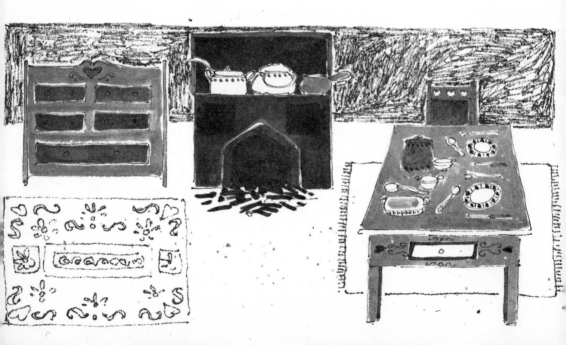

Poor tailor! His naughty bride had filled her pockets with peas, and when her husband had lighted her to bed, holding the candle as he went upstairs, she followed a little way behind, dropping peas all over the kitchen floor and the stairs.

Then she went to bed, thinking to herself, "Ha ha! Now the mannikins will fall over the peas and hurt themselves, and I shall find them in the morning."

And she went to sleep, feeling quite pleased with herself. That night the tailor heard a queer sound down in the kitchen and up the stairs—a sound like a swarm of angry bees.

"Leave the floor, brothers, never mind the dust,
Never mind the polishing, never mind the rust!
Leave each plate and dish and cup,
The peas she dropped she must clear up!
Leave the work, brothers, leave it all undone!
When peas are dropped to hurt us, we can't have any fun!"

The next day the tailor found that all his stitches had been unpicked, the house was dirty and the chimney full of soot.

And as for the mannikins, they never came back, and that poor little German village lost all its luck.

The Wonderful Bottle

(Irish)

It may well be that this story started in Ireland just over a hundred
years ago at the time of the Great Potato Famine when for four
years running, from 1845 to 1848, the potato crop failed and, as
this was the chief food there, especially of the poorer people,
thousands of families starved and very many died or fled from
their country to England and America.

Once upon a time, there was an Irishman whose name was Micky.
He was very poor, and he lived in a little mud hut with his wife, his
six little children, one pig, two or three chickens and a very old friend.
That old friend was the most valuable thing in the house. It was a cow.

It might seem an odd thing for the cow to be living in the house.
But, then, Micky was so poor that he did not even have a barn where
he could keep the cow, so in the daytime she just had to graze on the
common, and at night she came and slept in the hut with Micky and
the children, a fat pig and two or three chickens.

They were all fond of the cow. They called her Rosalind, and if you had told them that there were lots of cows far handsomer than Rosalind, and not half so skinny, they would not have believed you. They thought that Rosalind was the most beautiful cow in the world. As long as they had Rosalind they were happy. If they were hungry, she gave them milk; if they were cold at night, they lay down quite close to her side and she warmed them; if they were sad, she looked at them so lovingly out of her big brown eyes that they had to go and kiss her.

One year they were colder and hungrier and sadder than they had ever been before. It was one of those years when everything seemed to go wrong all at once. To begin with, the potato crop failed, and that meant there was very little to eat. Naturally, they had to have something, so they decided to sell the chickens. And then, what did those chickens do but, each and every one of them, die of the pip!

Poor Micky was in great distress. There was his wife looking thin and hungry, and all the children crying for bread. So now the only thing to do was to sell the pig. So Micky got up early one morning, went over to the piggy's part of the hut—oh!—Piggy was dead! She had caught the measles—or swine fever or something like that—and she was as dead as a door nail.

"It's no use standing there and doing nothing," said his wife. "You'll have to go to the fair and sell old Rosalind. Get up now, Micky. Put a rope round her neck, and take her off to the fair. And see that she fetches a good price."

At this all the children began to howl, and if Micky had stayed to wipe their eyes and blow their noses, he would never have got outside the door. And, as for Rosalind, she seemed to know all about it. She just looked round with her big sad eyes, gave a snuffling sigh, and ambled through the doorway and up the road towards the fair, with Micky behind her.

It was a long way to the fair, and Micky was very tired because he was hungry, but it was a nice sunny day, so he jogged along slowly, thinking of all the good food which he would buy when once he had sold Rosalind.

About mid-day, when the sun was high in the sky, he was astonished to see the cow stand stock still and stare up the road.

"Now then, Rosalind, old lady," he said, "the time's getting on. Come along now, you can't have a rest until you get to the fair."

He gave her a playful whack with a stick, but Rosalind didn't move; she still stared up the road.

"Now then! Now then!" said Micky, "I don't see anything. What's the matter with you, eh?"

But Rosalind took no notice; she still stared up the road, and presently she gave a loud, long "moo," flung her tail up in the air, took two little mincing steps forward and one back, for all the world like a dancing girl.

"Now then, now then!" said Micky. "What's the matter with you? You are bewitched! Here, Rosalind, old girl, keep quiet!"

But Rosalind continued to dance, and just as she had given Micky a flip with her tail, a squeaky little voice said, "Dear me! That's a very fine cow you have got there." And Micky looked down and saw a little old man at his side.

Such a peculiar little chap! He had an old, wrinkled yellow face, exactly like a dried cauliflower, a pointed nose as red as a beet, and tiny little twinkling eyes. Seeing him made Micky jump with fright. For there was Rosalind still dancing like a silly schoolgirl, and now this little old cauliflower gentleman seemed to have sprung up from nowhere.

"Good-day to you!" said Micky gruffly, and gave Rosalind a whack to make her go on.

"Good-day," squeaked the little man. "You're going to Cork Fair, *I* know. But you needn't, because *I'll* buy your cow."

Micky felt more cheerful, because he was rather tired, and he did not see why he should not sell Rosalind to the little old man, provided he could get a good price.

"What'll you give for her?" said he.

"This bottle," answered the old man, and he pulled an empty bottle out of his pocket.

At that Micky burst out laughing. "O-ho-ho-ho! An empty bottle!" said he. "And how do you suppose I'm going to feed my children on an empty bottle?"

"Micky O'Flanaghan," said the little man again, "give me the cow and take the bottle! Then go home. Clean up your house. Put the bottle on the floor and say, 'Bottle, do your duty.' This is the last time I

shall ask you. Remember, you've got a chance of being a rich man."

Micky was just going to say, "Get along with your nonsense, when Rosalind gave him an awful flip in the eye with her tail, and before he knew where he was, the cow and the little old man had disappeared, and he was alone in the road with the empty bottle in his hand.

Micky was more than a little bit nervous when he went home. He did not know what his wife would say; and he knew the children would cry when they saw that he had brought them an empty bottle instead of Rosalind.

However, he had to go home, so he hurried back to his little mud hut, and out came his wife and children to meet him.

Poor things, they did look so tired and hungry. "Well, well," they asked, "what have you got? Have you brought some food? How much money did you get for poor Rosalind?"

Micky blushed red. "Er-er!" he said, "I got a bottle."

"A bottle!" screamed his wife.

"A bottle!" cried the children. "He's sold Rosalind for a bottle. Oh-hoo-boo-hoo—he's sold Rosalind for a bottle," and they burst into tears.

Poor Micky felt miserable. However, he remembered what the little old man had said, and began to tidy up the house and to take no notice of all the sobbing and crying. Then he took the bottle out of his coat pocket, put it in the middle of the floor and said, "Bottle, do your duty!"

No sooner had he spoken than all the children stopped crying and shouted, "Daddy, Daddy, look!"

Out of the bottle jumped two little men, no bigger than the little gentleman with the cauliflower face. Before you could say "Hey presto!" they had spread the table with eggs and milk and bread and honey and meat and cheese, and then popped back into the bottle again.

Such excitement! And it was a splendid meal they all had!

They were never hungry again. And all because dear old Rosalind danced in the road when she saw a little old man with a cauliflower face!

What happened to that bottle? That was Micky's secret. No one ever knew.

Sing-Sun and the Tartar

(Chinese)

The Tartars came from Asia. They were ugly people, with flat faces and sloping eyes, and they travelled about in crowds or tribes, called hordes. When they went from place to place, they packed all their goods in carts with two wheels, and they lived in round felt tents. The women drove the carts, and the men walked beside them wearing armour, made of dried buffalo hide. They drank mare's milk, which they called Kumis, and when they had a meal they used to put out grease in front of their tents, in case the gods which they worshipped were hungry too.

You will find all sorts of interesting things about the Tartars in a book written by a famous traveller who lived nearly 700 years ago. It is called the *Journey of Messer Marco Polo,* the Venetian.

The Great Wall of China still exists. It is 1,500 miles long, and crosses mountains, valleys and rocks over the North of China. It was begun 300 years before the birth of Christ by an Emperor called Shi Hwang Ti, who was afraid of the Tartar hordes.

Once upon a time there was a nobleman—a Chinese mandarin whose name was Whang-ho. He had three daughters who were very pretty, but the youngest was the prettiest of all, and her name was Sing-Sun.

Every day Sing-Sun and her sisters used to look at their faces in the waters of a lake near the mandarin's garden. The water was as clear as glass, and deep down they could see the goldfish swimming.

One day they noticed that one of the goldfish was bigger and brighter than any of the others. "Look at him!" said Sing-Sun. "I'm sure he's wiser than any other fish in the lake. Let's speak to him!" "Oh *yes!*" said the others, "do let's!" and they put their little faces as close to the water as possible and called: "Honourable goldfish, come up and talk to us." And up popped the goldfish.

"Well, well, well!" said he, "and what may you be wanting this morning?"

"He-he-he! Ha-ha-ha!" laughed the little Chinese girls, opening their little coral mouths and showing their little white teeth, "are you wise, honourable goldfish, as wise as the mandarin, our father?"

"Well, well, well!" said the goldfish. "I don't know about that, but I'm fairly wise. I can tell fortunes, you know!"

"Oho!" cried the little Chinese maidens, nodding their little black heads. "He can tell fortunes." And they began to whisper together, and suddenly they all spoke at once "Please-tell-me-what-sort-of-man-I'm-going-to-marry! He-he-he-he-he! Ha-ha-ha-ha!" They laughed one after another like a chime of silver bells.

"Well, well, well," said the goldfish. "Is that all you want to know? It's easy! The eldest will marry a soldier. The second will marry a judge. But Sing-Sun will marry a prince."

"Oh, Sing-Sun," laughed the others, "he-he-he-he! ha-ha-ha-ha!"

"Ooooh! Honourable goldfish!" said Sing-Sun, looking rather shy. "What will he be like?"

"Aha," said the goldfish, "wait and see! But you must be kind to the Tartar, Sing-Sun, or you will never meet the prince. Good-bye!" And under the water he popped, and they did not see him again for months.

Sing-Sun was very much puzzled. She wanted to marry a prince, but she did not understand the advice about the Tartar. She knew that the Tartars were ugly, fierce men, who lived on the other side of China, but she had never seen one, and she could not understand what the goldfish meant.

One day, Whang-ho the mandarin, who was a very busy person, decided to go on a long journey. Before setting out he called to his three daughters and said: "I am going away for a long time. Be good girls and do as you are told, and I will bring you each a present when I come home."

The three little Chinese maidens clapped their hands.

"Honourable father," they said, "will you bring us just exactly what we asked for?"

"Of course I will," said the mandarin, and he pinched their cheeks.

"He-he-he-he!" laughed the eldest. "I want some golden slippers with jewels sewn all over the toes."

"Ha-ha-ha-ha!" giggled the second. "I want some combs for my hair, with a diamond in each as big as the lobe of my ear!"

"And what for you, Sing-Sun?" asked the mandarin.

Sing-Sun thought for a moment, and then she said, "For me a piece of the great wall of China!"

"Ooooh, Sing-Sun," said the others. They were frightened, for the great wall of China stretched from one end of the country to the other, and it had been built to keep out the Tartars, the country's enemies. What would happen if the mandarin made a hole in it?

"Oh, Sing-Sun!" said the mandarin, but he had promised to bring each daughter exactly what she had asked for, and, of course, he could not break his word.

Off he went, feeling very much worried.

When he had journeyed far and wide, he went to a great market and bought the slippers and the combs, and then he mounted his

pony and rode along by the great wall, looking and looking all the time for a place where it would be easy to break off a bit. At last he thought he saw a thin place. He jumped off his pony and gazed round stealthily! No one was looking. He crept up to the great wall—and—whang—he gave it an awful blow with a hammer. But he could not break it. He tried again. Whang-whang-whang! And again—bang-whop-whang! Out fell a large chunk and made a hole in the wall.

And then—and then—! Oh! Through the hole sprang a hideous Tartar, and grabbed the mandarin by the shoulder.

"Ho, ho!" said he, "now I've got into China, and you'll go through that hole into prison and I'll chop off your head."

"Oh dear, dear!" said the mandarin, "please don't do that. I meant no harm, dear Tartar, really I didn't! I was only getting a present for Sing-Sun!"

"Sing-Sun?" said the Tartar. "Who's Sing-Sun?"

"Ah," said the mandarin. "Sing-Sun is my youngest daughter, the most beautiful girl in China. She has hair like black silk, slanting eyes like almonds and lips like curved coral. What will happen to my little Sing-Sun if you cut off her father's head?"

"Well," said the Tartar, "I rather like the sound of Sing-Sun. I'll tell you what I'll do. If Sing-Sun will marry me, I'll set you free." So saying, the Tartar dragged the mandarin through the hole and shut him into a dark prison. Then he sprang into China, jumped on to the mandarin's pony and set out to find Sing-Sun.

He did not know the way to the mandarin's house—but the pony did! It trotted quickly all the way home, and the Tartar walked straight into the house and found Sing-Sun and her sisters drinking tea.

"Eeee! Aaa! Ooo!" screamed the three. "It's a Tartar!"

Then Sing-Sun remembered what the goldfish had said—"be kind to the Tartar or you'll never meet the prince"—so she gathered up her courage and said: "Honourable Tartar, won't you have some tea? A-and p-p-p-please tell us why you have come."

The Tartar sat down and drank the tea, and told how he had managed to get into China through the hole in the wall. When he had finished he said: "And now if Sing-Sun will marry me, I'll set your father free."

"Oh dear!" said Sing-Sun, and "Ooh, Sing-Sun," said the two sisters.

Well, of course, Sing-Sun did not want her father to remain in prison, and she kept thinking to herself: "If I'm kind to the Tartar, perhaps I shall meet the prince." So she did marry the Tartar, and he carried her right away to the hole in the great wall and took her to live in a tent.

Of course, he set her father free, and when the poor mandarin saw his lovely little Sing-Sun married to an ugly Tartar his hair grew quite white with sorrow. But he could not do anything. He could only kiss his daughter "Goodbye," and go back to his house by the lake.

Poor Sing-Sun was left all alone in the Tartar's tent, and, although he was always kind to her, she felt sad and lonely.

One day the Tartar was watching her as she sat inside the tent embroidering blue butterflies on a piece of flame-coloured silk. "Sing-Sun," he said, "I suppose you'll never learn to love me?" And two tears rolled down his ugly hairy cheeks and splashed on to his great brown hands.

When she saw him crying, Sing-Sun felt very sorry for him. He was always so kind to her that she did not want him to be unhappy. "Oh Tartar dear, don't cry," she said, "You're so good that I believe I'm beginning to love you already."

The Tartar looked up wistfully. "Do you think you will ever be able to give me a kiss?" he asked.

And Sing-Sun, before she really knew what she was doing, put her slender arms round his ugly short neck and gave him a little butterfly kiss on his hairy cheek.

Then the most wonderful thing happened. The air was suddenly filled with music, flowers blossomed in the grass, red, blue and yellow butterflies flitted in and out of the tent. Sing-Sun looked up in surprise and—the Tartar had disappeared. In his place there was the most beautiful prince. He led Sing-Sun out of the tent, through the hole in the great wall and back to China.

When they passed her father's house, both her sisters ran out, crying, "Ooh, Sing-Sun, what a lovely prince!" And just then the goldfish popped his head out of the lake and said, "Ah! So you *were* kind to the Tartar!"

And quite right he was, too: he *did* say, "You must be kind to the Tartar or you'll *never* meet the prince!"

One day when you are old and wise, perhaps it will all be clear to see.

Zarifa and the White Calf

(Algerian)

Zarifa's country, Algeria, was once called Barbary, and for hundreds of years it was the home of pirates who used to sail into the Mediterranean and attack ships.

The chief ruler of the Barbary States was known as the Dey of Algiers. It was a dey, Hussein, who lost his country to France.

It happened like this: the Algerian Government owed France some money. The French Consul, living in Algiers, went to talk to Dey Hussein about it. The weather was hot, and Dey Hussein had a "fly-swatter" in his hand. During the conversation he grew angry, lost his temper, and instead of using the "fly-swatter" for its proper purpose, he hit the French Consul with it.

This was considered an insult to the French nation. War was declared and in 1830 the town of Algiers surrendered to France. Algeria did not regain her independence until 1962.

Zarifa lived in Algeria, which is in the North of Africa. She was a wrinkled old crone, and she had a funny little white house with a flat roof. The floor of the house was just the bare earth stamped flat, and there Zarifa used to sleep with her grandchildren and her son and her son's wife, all huddled together on a mat made of grass.

But in the summer, when the days and nights were hot, old Zarifa would creep out of the house, put a ladder up against the wall and climb on to the flat roof, and there she would lie, looking up at the stars. And in the early morning, when the sun rose and the sky was beginning to get yellow, Zarifa would rise too and begin to pick over the grains of corn which lay in a heap on the roof. This was necessary because she was going to make bread, and before she could do that she had to see that no bits of mould or stone were hidden among the grains of corn. Then she had to take the clean grains and crush them between two heavy stones so as to make flour. And that flour she would make into little thin cakes of coarse bread and take them on a tray on her head to the town baker, who put them in his oven and baked them for Zarifa and her grandchildren and her son and her

127

son's wife. When they were ready, Zarifa would put the tray on her head and carry the hot loaves home, and the family would all have breakfast.

Old Zarifa would look round and think how big and strong and well her son was; how plump and pretty her son's wife was, and what lovely fat little dumplings of grandchildren she had. And she would feel very contented and happy.

But, unhappily, a day came when all that changed. The wrinkled old face of Zarifa began to look sad and more wrinkled than ever. Her skin was like a withered leaf, and the light went out of her eyes. Her son's cheeks began to grow hollow and his face pale. Her son's wife sat listlessly in the cottage and her flesh seemed scarcely to cover her bones, she was so thin; and as for the lovely fat little dumplings of grandchildren; they seemed to have disappeared, and in their places were four little haggard creatures whose ribs you could count.

There was no corn on the roof now. Zarifa very seldom went to the baker's with loaves of bread. On the way home she never met a goat or a cow, but only some poor, thin, hungry neighbour. It was terrible.

The cause of this was a war in the land, and the town in which Zarifa lived was being besieged. The enemy surrounded it. No one could get out to fetch food. The cattle and flocks which used to graze outside

the walls had been taken by the enemy, and the few poor creatures which people used to keep in their back yards had long ago been eaten up. The town was starving.

At last the mayor sent for his messenger. "Go," said he, "and climb to the top of the minaret outside the mosque" (that was the place where people said their prayers), "and call all the people together."

So the messenger went to the mosque, mounted the stairs up to the minaret and called north, south, east and west, "Good people!

Come to the mosque. Good people, come to the mosque!"

Out of the houses came the people, very sad and very quiet, very thin, pale and hollow-eyed. Some could scarcely stand on their feet, and some were weeping.

"O my father," said one woman to the mayor, "can you not give us bread for our little ones?"

"O mayor," cried another, "can nothing be done to drive the enemy from our gates? We shall die if we cannot get food."

"Alas, good people!" said the mayor. "I can do nothing. We must surrender. There is scarcely any food left. We cannot hope to save the town."

For a minute there was silence.

"Is it agreed?" asked the mayor. "Shall we give up the town?"

"Yes! Yes!" murmured the people. "Give it up! How can we hold it?"

They turned away. But Zarifa did not turn away. She walked up to the mayor trembling with anger. She shook her skinny fist at him and croaked with rage like an old frog.

"Give up the town to the enemy!" she shrieked. "Where is your courage, you white-livered sons of dogs? Give me but my will and I'll save the town."

Everybody stared at the old woman in amazement.

"O my mother," said the mayor, for that is the way a young man speaks to an old lady in the East. "O my mother, we would willingly save the town if only we knew how."

"Do as I tell you, my son," said the old woman. "Bring me a calf."

"Calf!" cried all the people. "Calf! why surely she is mad! All the calves in the place were eaten long ago!"

But Zarifa was obstinate. "I must have a calf," she said. And she was so persistent that at last the mayor sent some messengers to look for one.

High and low they sought, and presently, to everyone's great delight, they returned dragging a small white calf by a rope. They had found it in the woodland of an old miser, who had hidden enough food to keep the calf quite sleek and fat. *He meant to sell it for a huge price when there was no more food in the town.*

"Give me my calf! Give me my calf!" whimpered the old man. But Zarifa took no notice. She looked round at all the people and said, "Bring me some corn!"

"Corn, corn! She, asking for corn! Why, Zarifa, there isn't more than a spoonful in any house."

"Then bring me the spoonfuls," shouted Zarifa angrily.

The people crept back to their houses and opened their corn bins. Some had a handful, some a spoonful, and some only a few grains of corn, but they brought what they had, and they looked at it sorrowfully and hungrily.

"Put it into a pail," said Zarifa.

Each person did as he was told, and when all had finished the pail
was nearly full.

Zarifa poured some water into it and mixed it into a sort of mash,
then she took it up to the calf, and, of course, as soon as the calf smelt
it, he put his nose into it and gobbled it up.

"Oh dear! Alas!" cried the people, "what have you done, Zarifa?
You've given the last corn in the town to the calf. You wicked old
woman to waste food on a fat calf when the children are starving!"

They were so angry with Zarifa that they would certainly have hurt
her if the mayor had not interfered.

"Let her alone! Let her alone!" said he. "She has promised to save
the town. Let us see what she will do."

"Take me to the city gates," said Zarifa. "Open them and let the calf out."

The mayor was greatly astonished at this extraordinary command. He hardly liked to open the gates when the enemy was outside, but Zarifa was stamping her foot and getting so angry that at last he went with her to the city gates, opened them just wide enough for the calf to pass through, drove the little creature out, and shut them again with a clang.

"And now, oh my children," said Zarifa, "return to your homes. To-morrow the city will be saved," and she hobbled back to the little flat-roofed house with her son, her son's wife and her four hungry grandchildren.

Then the little calf did what most calves would have done. It trotted over to the nearest patch of grass and began to nibble it.

Meanwhile the king and his soldiers who were besieging the city could hardly believe their eyes. A fat little calf eating grass!

"Tut, tut," said the king, "they can't be as hungry as we are if they let a fat calf out to graze. By this time they ought to have eaten every animal in the place. They ought to be starving."

"Yes, oh mighty king!" said his officers. "Surely it is very strange. But we pray you let us catch the calf and eat it ourselves, for we are so hungry."

The king gave them permission and they caught the calf. But judge of their astonishment when they found inside it a quantity of undigested corn.

"Oh king, oh mighty king!" they cried. "These people are not starving. See, there is undigested corn inside this calf. If they can afford to give corn to their cattle, they must have plenty to spare. We might as well besiege the moon!"

They turned away, looking greatly distressed. Presently they began to murmur among themselves, grumbling that they were hungry and they would not go on besieging a city which was full of food.

When the king looked at their angry, threatening faces, he was afraid. "So be it," he said, "pick up the tents; prepare the chariots and the horses. To starve a city which feeds its calves on corn will take us months."

So the order was given, and by the morning the enemy had gone. And when old Zarifa climbed on to the roof of her little white house, there was no sign of a soldier outside the city walls.

And that was how an old Arab grandmother saved her native town.

The Leprechaun
and the Scarlet Garters

(Irish)

Some people say that in the old days the Irish used to call the leprechaun a "lucorpan", from a word, "lu", meaning little, and "corp", meaning body; that is to say, "the little-bodied one".

There are all sorts of tales about "the little-bodied one", and in every story he is a shoemaker, and he has either a hidden crock of gold or a magic purse which always has a shilling in it.

There was once a boy whose name was Pat Fitzpatrick. He was an Irish boy, and he lived with his mother, a donkey and a pig in a little bit of a mud hut at the foot of a hill. There was a wooden fence round the hut, and a potato patch, where the chickens scratched in the day-time, and nothing else—not even a wooden coop for the fowls; so at night *they* had to come into the hut, and Pat Fitzpatrick and his mother slept on one side, and the chickens and the donkey and the pig on the other. And they found it a very comfortable arrangement.

Every night Pat's mother used to kneel in front of the fire and blow the peat into a delicious sweet-smelling glow; then she would take two sacks of straw and Pat would put his head on one and she would put her head on the other, and they would both put their feet towards the fire and go to sleep.

Every morning when she awoke, the mother would blow up the fire and make porridge. And when it was ready she would shake Pat by the shoulder, crying, "Get up, ye lazy loon! You'll never catch a leprechaun with your eyes shut. Remember the crock of gold!" As soon as she said that, Pat jumped up, swallowed his porridge and ran out of the hut to look for the leprechaun and the crock of gold.

Pat knew what a leprechaun was; a leprechaun was a fairy shoemaker —a tiny little cobbler no bigger than the palm of a hand. There were lots of leprechauns, and they all made shoes for the fairies. They lived under the ground among the roots of the trees and the rabbit holes, and they were very rich. They had a crock full of gold. In every different part of the country where the leprechauns lived, there was always a crock of gold, hidden under a thornbush, or deep in the ground, where it could not be seen.

Pat Fitzpatrick and his mother knew that there was a big family of leprechauns somewhere near their hut, because they used to hear the tap-tap-tap of tiny hammers and the thin squeaky sound of needles and thread being pulled in and out of leather. But they never set eyes on the leprechauns themselves. Mrs. Fitzpatrick used to wag her finger at Pat every morning and say, "If ever you get a glimpse of a leprechaun, don't take your eyes off it, or it will disappear, the rascal!" And Pat used to say, "I'll remember, Mother," and he would go off and spend the day hunting for the crock of gold.

Of course, Pat had no business to go looking for that crock of gold. It belonged to the leprechauns, and not to him. But, alas, he was not a very honest boy. He didn't think about the leprechauns. He just said to himself, "If I can find that crock of gold I shall be rich for ever," and went on looking for it.

One day when Pat was returning in the evening, feeling very cross and tired after his search, he heard, quite close to his foot, the tap-tap-tap of a tiny hammer and the squeaky sound of thread being drawn through leather. He looked down, and there was a leprechaun making a fairy shoe. The leprechaun was so busy that he didn't see Pat, and went on stitching away and humming a little tune. Pat very nearly ran home to tell his mother, but he suddenly remembered that, if you take your eyes off a leprechaun, it disappears; so he stayed where he was and stared. The leprechaun was such a funny little fellow—all hairy and quite old and wrinkled. He was wearing a little red cap with a tassel, and a leather apron, and a really perfect little pair of hobnailed shoes. He sat there quite seriously tap-tap-tapping and stitch-stitch-stitching, so intent on his work that he did not see Pat.

Then Pat very carefully stretched out his hand and *grab!* he seized the leprechaun, apron, hammer, shoe and all. How he squeaked! He spat and struggled and scratched like an angry cat, but Pat held on and never took his eyes off the little creature, in case he should disappear.

"Aha, ye little struggling crosspatch! I've got ye," said Pat. "Now you tell me—" (he gave the leprechaun a shake), "you tell me where's that crock of gold."

The poor little leprechaun grew quite pale. He began to shiver and shake. "What's that?" he said, "g-g-gold, what g-gold?"

"Now, now, now," said Pat, "you know quite well what I mean. *Where's that crock of gold?*"

"E-e-e!" screeched the leprechaun, giving a sudden jump, "Look behind you, Pat. The cow's in the corn."

Pat gave a yell and very nearly

looked behind him, but remembered just in time: if you take your eyes off a leprechaun it disappears.

"Ah, ye little rascal," said he, "don't you be up to your tricks with me! Stop scratching, will ye! I'm not going to let ye go, and I'm not going to take my eyes off you till you show me the crock of gold."

"Don't know *where* it is!" growled the leprechaun. He was so frightened that all his hair stood on end and pricked Pat like anything, but Pat wouldn't let go and he wouldn't take his eyes off the leprechaun.

"Now then," said he, giving the leprechaun a shake till his teeth rattled, "out with it. Where's that crock of gold?"

"Hidden!" screamed the leprechaun. "And you shan't have it, so there! E-e-e! Look out, Pat, your house is burning!"

"Bad luck to you, you ill-mannered little villain," said Pat. "I'll not take my eyes off you, whatever you say. Now then, where's that crock of gold?"

"If I tell you, will you let me go?" asked the leprechaun.

"I'll not let you go till you *show* me where that crock of gold is hidden," said Pat. "I'll not take my eyes off you, either. So you'd better be quick. Come along now. Do as you're told."

The poor leprechaun wriggled in Pat's hand, and two large tears rolled down his hairy cheeks. "I wish you wouldn't hold so tight," he whimpered, "you're squashing me to a jelly. Let *go!*"

"Not I," said Pat. "I'll not let you go, young fellow, till you show me where the crock of gold is hidden."

"Oh, all right! Have it your own way," said the leprechaun grumpily. "I'll show you. And then I hope you'll enjoy it when you get it. Come on!" He wriggled around in Pat's hand and pointed to the hill.

"Over the hill?" asked Pat.

"Yes," said the leprechaun, "over the hill and then through the bog —then turn to your right through the wood and to your left across the brook, and to your right over—"

"Ah! Would you try to fool me?" said Pat. "You know quite well it's much nearer than that. You give those instructions properly or 'I'll squeeze the life out of you. Do you hear?" And Pat shook the poor little leprechaun till he grew red in the face and gasped for breath. "Huh! huh! huh!" he panted. "Put me down, Pat, and I'll show you, I promise."

Pat held on to the leprechaun with one hand and took off his braces with the other. Then he tied the leprechaun round the middle and held the end of the braces and let the little cobbler walk. Walk? It was more like a gallop! That leprechaun ran like a hare, with Pat hanging on and following—bumpetty-bump over the stones, slip-slither in the wet moss, slush-slush-slush through the bogs, stumble, scratch, bang, bump! Pat hung on like grim death, and the leprechaun tore along through the worst places possible. It was terrible for Pat, because he never dared take his eyes off the leprechaun. He just followed helter-

skelter till—bump!—the leprechaun suddenly stopped short, and Pat found himself in front of a field of thistles.

"*Now* will you let me go?" asked the leprechaun.

"Where's that crock of gold?" asked Pat.

"*There!*" screamed the leprechaun, and Pat was so excited that he nearly took his eyes off the little fellow, but he remembered just in time.

"Now then, you little rascal, take me up to it or I'll—"

"All right, all right," said the leprechaun, "*there,* under the ground under that thistle. And you'll have to go back and get a spade or you'll never be able to dig it up. Aha!" And he began to dance up and down and chuckle with glee. "You'll never remember which thistle, Pat—the whole field is full of them."

"So *that's* it, is it?" said Pat. "I'll remember easily enough, thank you!" And so saying, he threw his scarlet woollen garter over the thistle.

"And now I'll go back and get the spade."

And then he picked up the leprechaun, braces and all, and put him in his pocket. But when, a moment later, he put in his hand to feel for him——he——he wasn't there! Pat had taken his eyes off the leprechaun and he had vanished—vanished with Pat's braces, too!

At first Pat was annoyed, but soon he said to himself, "Good riddance! Anyhow, I know where the crock of gold is."

He ran home as fast as his legs could carry him; he didn't even stop to tell his mother. He just seized a spade and raced back to the field of thistles—and looked—and then—

And then he sat right down on the grass and howled! "Ooo-hoo-hoo! Oh, hoo-hoo! *Why* did I take my eyes off him—ooh-hoo!" Because on every single thistle there was a scarlet garter, and down under the ground Pat heard the tap-tap-tap of tiny hammers and the squeak of thread being drawn through leather.

Pat never again saw a leprechaun, and he never found the crock of gold, and of course after that everyone laughed at him because he had only one garter, and had to tie his trousers up with string.

Reynard the Fox and his Uncle Bruin the Bear

(Northern European)

Long ago it was not so easy to get books as it is today, for they were all written by hand. Knowing how long it takes to write a page or even a line, it is easy to understand how much patience and toil went into the making of books.

Most of the book-making was done by monks, who used to sit in little cells carefully copying. They made beautiful letters, colouring in the capitals with bright inks and paints. Their fingers grew stiff and their eyes tired, but still they worked.

At last some clever men who lived in Flanders invented a printing press. This meant that books could be made far more quickly, and everyone was very much excited.

An Englishman, called William Caxton, who lived in Bruges, learned how to print, and set up a press in a shop in London about 500 years ago. He knew the Flemish language very well, and one of the books which he translated from it and printed was the history of Reynard the Fox.

Many people now rather like foxes, but there was a time when even the members of the animal kingdom were very angry with the fox. The fact of the matter was he played such pranks that he made them *tired*. And when they tried to make him suffer for his naughtiness, he was so cunning that he just wriggled out of every punishment. There was no holding back Master Reynard. Reynard was the fox's name, for in those days, it is said, all the animals called one another by names. Just as people don't call each other "child" or "boy" or "girl," but each has a special name, so had the animals.

The lion was called *Noble*. He was the king of all the beasts, and the the others were a little bit afraid of him. The cock was called *Chanticleer,* which means "the clear singer." They called him that because he used to sing out in a clear voice every morning at sunrise, so that all the birds and the beasts would know when to wake up.

And there was a *bear* there too. He was called Bruin, and he was a sort of policeman. Of course the animals had to have a policeman, and it was Bruin's job to come and fetch them away when the king said they were to go to prison. He made a very grumpy, growly policeman.

But Reynard the fox didn't mind him a bit! Bruin was his uncle, and when the bear came galumphing along and growled out, "Now then, move along there, please," Reynard just sat back on his haunches and laughed behind his paw, which was being very disrespectful to a policeman.

So Reynard went on playing pranks just as though there were no such thing as a policeman to take him to prison, and at last matters grew from bad to worse, and the animals made up their minds to have a meeting and decide what was to be done with Master Reynard.

Of course, Chanticleer came first. He had to call all the others.

"Cock-a-doodle-do!" After him, looking rather fussy and hysterical, came all his wives, cackling away, all of them edging this way and that so as to get the best seats, and taking such a long time to make up their minds that the other animals got in first.

There was a badger, an otter, a tiger, a jackal. There was a horse, a donkey, a mule, a weasel, a rabbit, a ferret—animals of all sorts. And there was old Bruin trying to keep order in this rabble. Everybody was talking at once, and *nobody* would stop, until Chanticleer lifted up his voice and shouted, "That'll doodle do!" Then there was some sort of order and the meeting began.

What a racket! You could hardly have believed your ears. Every single one of those animals had a complaint to make about Reynard! And, what's more, everything they said was quite true. Nobody had a good word for the fox. He had disturbed everybody's family life. He killed! He stole! He played tricks! In fact, he had broken every law in the animal world, and the result was that he must come before the king for his trial. When an animal was to be brought before the king, it meant something serious was going to happen, and so old Bruin Bear was sent to fetch the culprit.

In the meantime, Reynard was hiding. He hid in the woods behind a great boulder. He knew well enough what all the bother was about, and when he peeped round the boulder and saw Bruin coming, he

laughed behind his paw and slipped back into his hiding-place. Bruin came straight on towards him. "Reynard," he growled, "it's no use your hiding. *I* see you behind that boulder. You just come along with me to stand your trial." He walked boldly up to the rock, looked behind it, and there was Reynard, lying on the ground with his eyes closed, and groaning as though he were in awful pain!

"Hey," said the bear. "What's the matter with *you*? Have you got the toothache? Have you been sick?"

"Oh, Uncle Bruin!" moaned the fox. "I'm very ill. I've been so silly. I've been eating honeycombs!"

"Ha! Honeycombs," said Bruin, and he pricked up his ears—all bears love honey! And old policeman Bruin simply couldn't resist it. "Honey, Reynard?" said he, "did you say honeycombs? Now where may they be?"

"Aah!" said Reynard, and his wicked little eyes twinkled, "I can show you where to find the best honey in the land. But you must walk slowly and let me lean on your shoulder, because, you see, I'm not very well yet!" "That's all right, Reynard," said Bruin. "I won't go very fast. It's very good of you to show me the way, but you'll have to come with me afterwards, you know. You must stand your trial."

"I know," said Reynard, and he pretended to look very sad, "but the honey isn't far away. We've just got time to go there first."

He limped along beside Bruin, and all the time he talked about honey until the old bear's mouth watered and he licked his lips.

Very soon the two animals came to a carpenter's yard. Mr. and Mrs. Carpenter and all their neighbours were indoors having dinner, so there was no one about, and Reynard led the way into the empty yard, and walked straight up to a large hollow log. Now in the log there was a crack which the carpenter had kept open by wedges. It was a wide crack, and Reynard put his head into it. "Here you are!" he said.

"The honey's quite safe. Poke your head in, Uncle Bruin, and look."

The bear was fearfully excited. He pushed Reynard out of the way, stood up on his hind legs with his fore-paws on the log, and poked his head into the crack.

No sooner had he done so, than Reynard pulled out the wooden wedges and the crack closed up with Bruin's head inside.

"I can't find any honey," growled Bruin. "This is a trick." He tried to pull out his head, but he was caught fast and couldn't move. He could just hear Reynard's voice in the distance, crying, "Hope you'll enjoy your honey, Uncle Bruin."

That bear was furious! He grumbled and growled and stamped. He gnashed his teeth and he howled with rage. But he couldn't get his head out, and every time he howled, a voice cried, "I hope you're enjoying your honey, Uncle Bruin."

Naturally, that made the bear angrier than ever, and he made such a noise that he roused the carpenter and his neighbours.

"Hi! hi! A bear, a bear!" they cried, and they came running out of their houses with sticks and rakes and pitchforks, and they all began to beat poor Bruin. And all he could do was to go on howling because he was still stuck fast, and all the time that he was getting more and more bruised, a nasty little voice from the forest cried, "Hope you're enjoying your honey, Uncle Bruin."

It was almost more than Bruin could stand.

He gave a terrific pull, burst the log in half and galloped as hard as he could into the forest, with the carpenter and the carpenter's wife and the carpenter's children and the neighbours and the neighbours' wives and the neighbours' children, all running after him with sticks and stones and all shouting, "Hi-yi! Hi-yi! A bear, a bear!"

Nobody but the bear heard a polite little voice asking, "Did you enjoy your honey, Uncle Bruin?"

Bruin knew whose voice it was, but he didn't know where the voice came from. Reynard had gone into hiding. *He* wasn't going to be taken to trial by a silly old bear-policeman.

Reynard had just played another of his pranks and got off scot-free.

Reynard the Fox and his Cousin Tybert the Cat

(Northern European)

This story is another part of the history of Reynard the Fox. Nobody knows who first told these stories nor where they come from. Perhaps, like the fairy-tales, they have been great travellers, for there are stories of talking animals in India and other Eastern countries, as well as in Europe. The best-known European ones are probably those told by Aesop, an ugly, deformed Greek slave who lived more than 2,500 years ago and who entertained everyone with his animal conversations. But he did not write his stories. He told them over and over again, so that people remembered them, and repeated them to their children, and their grandchildren. Two hundred years after Aesop died, somebody collected his stories, which are called fables, and wrote them in a book.

The Reynard stories and some others which seem to belong only in Flanders, the North of France and the West of Germany, are Beast stories unlike all others in being connected into one long history with a special animal, like Reynard, as hero.

This animal story happened long ago in the good old days when the animals knew one another as well as one knows one's neighbours. Some of them were good friends, and some of them were not.

But in the days when Reynard the Fox was alive, *nobody* liked him— not even his own relatives—because he was so mischievous. No one knew why, but on every possible occasion, he seemed to be playing some trick on somebody. At last matters came to such a pass that the animals all complained to the king, Noble the lion. Noble did not take much notice of the first complaint, or of the second, but when a third animal came, he began to think it serious. And when he found that, one after another, every creature in the kingdom was complaining about Reynard, he thought it was time to *do* something.

So he called a meeting. Every animal came to it except Reynard, but *he* wasn't going to be caught so easily as that. Not he!

Well, since Reynard wouldn't come, the king said he must be fetched. One after another, the animals were chosen to be policemen, but none of them managed to catch Reynard. He either slipped away when he saw them coming or he went to meet them, all smiles and good manners, and then played some dreadful trick which sent them back to their homes, howling with rage.

At last it was the cat's turn. The cat's name was Tybert. He was the fox's cousin, and, on the whole, the two were quite good friends. "Look here, Tybert," said the king. "It's your turn to be policeman. Now, listen to me. Go straight to Reynard's house. Knock at the door and tell him to follow you to the meeting. I know Reynard is your cousin and rather a good friend of yours. If he won't obey at once, just try and coax him."

Poor Tybert did not like the idea at all. He put his two paws in front of his face and cried, "Mi-aou! What shall I do? I am only a poor weak little puss. If Uncle Bruin Bear couldn't fetch Reynard, how can I?"

"I am afraid I don't know," said the king. "Anyhow, it is your turn, so you must do the best you can. Now, Tybert, don't be a coward. Go along at once."

"Mi-aou," said Tybert, and as he bowed to the king the tears ran down his fur coat.

Off he went, very slowly, in the direction of Reynard's house. He *did* feel nervous. His whiskers all went limp, and the rest of his hair stood out like bristles. He was really so frightened that he could not walk straight and did nothing but wave his tail in the air.

Of course, Reynard saw him coming. His cunning little eyes were

always open. He just peeped out of his door and saw Tybert in the distance.

"Hallo! Hallo!" said Reynard to himself. "I *do* believe they've sent cousin Tybert as a policeman." He put his paw in front of his mouth and tittered. Then off he started as bold as brass to meet Tybert.

"Good morning, Tybert, old fellow!" said he. "Dear, dear, dear! You don't look at all well. Come along in and let's have a little talk. I can't tell you how pleased I am to see you."

Tybert felt rather cheered by this, and he began to purr a little, but still, he had to do his duty, so he stood stock-still in the middle of the path and began to speak very solemnly. "Mi-aou," he said, "I've a very unpleasant task, Cousin Reynard. I've been sent by the king to bring you to judgment. Mi-aou, Cousin Reynard, do come quietly, b-b-because I'm v-very fond of you, and I wouldn't like to scratch you."

After that he stopped because he was really very nervous, and he felt his whiskers getting all limp again.

"Quietly!" said Reynard. "Of course I'll come quietly. My dear little Tybert, I'm so fond of you, I'd go anywhere with you. But don't let's go yet. You look tired and hungry. Come and sit down for a few minutes. We'll have a little bit of something to eat and then we'll set off."

"That's very kind of you Reynard," said Tybert. "I really *am* rather hungry. Er, Reynard—is-is there such a thing as a mouse about the place?"

"A mouse," said Reynard. "Of course! Of course, dozens of great big fat ones! Come along, Tybert. I'll give you the best meal that you've ever had."

Reynard led the way through the woods and out into an open space where there was a little house in a pretty garden and, not far away, a barn. This was the home of a schoolmaster, who lived there with his wife and children. They had a cow, and several chickens and a nice field of corn. In the winter they stored the grain on one side of the barn and allowed the chickens to sleep on the other. And well did Master Reynard know that. Only two nights ago he had crept into the barn and stolen a chicken for his supper. He actually laughed behind his paw when he thought of it, but he was really laughing at something else. He was laughing at something he had suddenly remembered— a trap. *He* knew that the schoolmaster had set a trap just in the doorway of the barn, because early that morning he had been listening behind the door. (That was one of Reynard's unpleasant habits. He was a little bit sneaky.) He had listened behind the door and he had heard the schoolmaster say to his wife, "That rascally fox (the old thief) has been at the chickens again. I've set a trap which will teach him better manners, once and for all." Then he had come out and Reynard had nipped behind the barn, just in time, and when the schoolmaster had returned to the house that fox sat down and shook with laughter. He threw up his two front paws, waved his brush and simply barked. Then he scampered off for fear someone should hear him.

Reynard grinned when he thought of it.

"What are you smiling at, Reynard?" asked Tybert.

"I'm smiling because it makes me so happy to think of that nice fat mouse, Cousin Tybert."

"Mi-aou," said Tybert, and he stretched his claws and licked his lips. "Where is it, Reynard? I'm very hungry."

"I'm glad to hear that," said Reynard, "because that means that you'll enjoy the meal. Here we are! Just wriggle through that hole in the barn door very quietly, then give a pounce, and you'll find it waiting for you. A lovely surprise, Tybert, dear."

Tybert went softly up to the barn door, put his nose down to the hole and wriggled through. Clap! BANG! WHACK! Down came the trap door and he was caught! He couldn't get out! He wriggled and he wriggled and he squirmed and he rolled. But he was caught.

"Mi-aou! Mi-aou! Come and help me, Reynard! Oh, Oh, Reynard, dear, I can't get out!"

"What did you say, Cousin Tybert? He's a nice fat mouse! Oh! I'm so glad."

"Mi-aou, Mi-aou! I can't get out!"

"I hope you're chewing it well. Don't swallow it whole or you'll get a pain, Tybert. Bite it up into little bits."

"Mi-aou, Reynard, I'm in a trap."

Reynard began to snigger. "Isn't that a surprise, Tybert," said he. "You never expected a mouse like *that*. I hope you're enjoying your meal, Cousin Tybert."

Then, at last, Tybert knew that he had been tricked. And he was furious. He kicked and plunged and rolled and wriggled. He mewed and he yowled with rage. He made such a noise that the cock woke up and began to crow, and that made the hens think it was morning and they all began to cluck. And when they began to cluck, the schoolmaster woke up and shouted, "The fox is in the hen house," and ran out in his nightshirt. And so, the cat yowled, the cock crowed, the hens clucked, the schoolmaster shouted, the schoolmaster's wife seized a broom to beat the fox, and the schoolmaster's little boy jumped clean out of the window shouting, "Me too!" and the baby fell out of the cradle and bumped its head and bellowed louder than all of them put together.

And in the midst of all this noise a voice said very politely, "I hope it's a nice fat mouse, Cousin Tybert."

But poor Tybert could not speak, for the schoolmaster had opened the barn door and was beating him with a broom, and all the chickens were flapping their wings and squawking. The schoolmaster's wife was shouting, "Take that, you old thief!" And the little boy screamed, "Where's the chicken you stole?" and outside a very polite voice kept on asking, "Are you enjoying the mouse, Cousin Tybert?"

At last Tybert became so angry that he collected all his strength and he gave the schoolmaster such a terribly bad scratch that the poor man fell down on the floor of the barn in a faint, and his wife and little boy had to run back for some water. Then Tybert bit and scratched and gnawed till he managed to break through the trap and wriggle out.

He did not waste any time! He just turned and ran as fast as he could. And as he shot out of the barn door he still heard a very kind, polite voice saying, "Are you after another mouse, Cousin Tybert?"

And that was the end of Tybert's adventure. It is doubtful if he ever attempted to take Reynard to a meeting again.

As for Reynard, as usual, he just sat back and shook with laughter.

The Magic Teakettle

(Japanese)

We do not know just when or where the kettle danced but it must surely have done so at the two festivals especially for children. One of these is Children's Day, the fifth day of the fifth month. The family prepares for several days. Shelves are put against the wall and covered with green cloth. Swords, helmets and bits of armour are put on them, and when the great day comes, a pole is set up in the garden and from its top floats a large cloth or paper fish with its mouth open. This fish is a carp, and it is chosen for the boys' festival because it swims upstream and leaps over waterfalls. Like the carp, a boy must swim up the stream of life and overcome all difficulties. When the festival is over the little Japanese boy eats a cake made of bean paste, and takes a hot bath in which iris blossoms have been steeped.

The girls' holiday is on March 3rd. It is called Hina-Matsuri which means the Festival of Dolls. In this case the shelves are filled with dolls. There are two at the top which represent the Emperor and the Empress. Below are three ladies of the court and two ministers and lower still five court musicians. Then come dolls of every size and shape, and on the bottom shelves toy cooking pots and dolls' furniture. The house is decorated with peach blossom, and at night candles are lighted. Cakes and sweet wine are given to the little girls, who pretend to feed their dolls. The children have great fun at this festival, but it is not all play. It is meant to teach them the importance of being good mothers and housewives, and the respect which they owe to the Emperor and the Empress.

This is a Japanese story, about a kettle. (Well, perhaps not exactly a kettle.) This story is also about an animal; at least, well—no, not exactly an animal, but—well, here's the story.

Once upon a time there was a temple in Japan, where a priest lived with a number of young men who were learning how to be priests, too. It was a very pretty temple, on the side of a hill where a little stream flowed. And in that stream there were silver fish and very clear sparkling water. Every morning the priest used to go to this stream to fill his kettle so as to make tea, and catch a little fish on the end of a rod.

One day, when he had caught his fish as usual, and filled his kettle, he was climbing up the hill and back to the temple, when he felt what *he* thought were drops of rain on his foot. He looked up at the sky, but there were no clouds, and he felt nothing on his face. He listened. "Drip-drip-drip!" "Drop-drop-drop," then faster, "Drip-drop! Drip-drop!" His foot was getting quite wet. He could not understand it. Suddenly he looked at his kettle and saw that it was only half full. It was leaking, leaking all round the edge. Somebody must have been careless and knocked it against something sharp, then hung it up in the temple without telling the priest.

"Tut, tut, tut!" said the priest crossly. "Now I shall have to fill another kettle, and I don't believe I've got one."

He climbed the hill as quickly as he could, hoping to save some of the water, but when he reached the temple, the kettle was empty and he could not have any tea. He felt rather tired after his walk, but he knew that the others would want some tea, so he began to hunt about for a kettle. At first he could not find one anywhere, but at last he remembered that, hanging on a hook high up in a corner, was a very,

very old one—an earthenware kettle which had been there for years and years and years. In fact, nobody could remember when it had not been there, and that is really why the priest had forgotten it, he was so used to it.

"Well, well, well!" said he. "Fancy my forgetting you—when you've been there all these years! Come along!" He climbed on to a stool, unhooked the kettle, blew a cloud of dust off the top of it and once again set out for the stream.

It took him a little time to come home, because he had to wash the kettle thoroughly before filling it. Also it was a good bit bigger than the other one, so it was quite heavy. Naturally the priest was quite glad to get back to the temple.

He sat on a reed mat on the floor and thought, "Now for a good cup of tea!"

He blew up the charcoal embers on the hearth, fixed up a little three-legged arrangement on which he used to stand his kettle, and began to boil the water.

And *then* something happened!

It was no laughing matter, because really it was very serious. *The kettle grew a tail!* A great big hairy one. It sprouted out of the side where the spout was, and began to move very slowly backwards and forwards. Wiggle-waggle! Wiggle-waggle! The priest was simply terrified. At first he thought that something had gone wrong with his own sight. He rubbed his eyes and looked again, and there was the kettle going bubble-bubble, bubble-bubble, and the tail going wiggle-waggle, wiggle-waggle. "Ay yi-yi!" shouted the priest. "Help! help!"

There was a patter-patter-patter of bare feet across the bamboo floor, and in ran one of the priest's pupils. "Oh dear! Oh dear! What *has* happened?" asked the pupil. "Are you ill, dear master?" But the priest could do nothing but point weakly at the kettle and whimper, "It's got a t-t-tail!" Then all the priest's pupils came running in and looked at the kettle and began to scream at once. One cried "Oh-oh!" Another cried, "Ah-ah!" and another "Ee-ee!" and another "Ii-Ii!" Clatter, clatter, clatter. And all the time the tail went slowly to and fro, wiggle-waggle, wiggle-waggle.

The priest's pupils were pale with horror, but just as they were calming down and wondering what to do, a change came over the kettle. The tail went faster, wiggle-waggle, wiggle-waggle, wiggle-waggle! The water inside boiled furiously, bubble-bubble-bubble, and on the side opposite the tail a large crack suddenly appeared.

It was not water which came out, but a *nose!* And after the nose came a whole head. A hairy head with brown beady eyes and sharp white teeth. It was the head of a badger.

Now, what can one do with a kettle with a hairy tail and a badger's head?

Of course, the priest and all his pupils began to scream again.

Then they began Ah-ahing and Ee-ee-ing and Ii-ii-ing and Oh-ohing! The scene might have been in the Zoo instead of a Japanese temple. It was so noisy that it frightened the kettle—or the badger—or what? The badger-kettle! The water went bubble-bubble, and the tail went wiggle-waggle, and the teeth went snip-snap, and that kettle jumped clean off the fire and began careering round the room. Whee-oo!

It was awful. "Oh-oh! Ah-ah! Ee-ee! Ii-ii!" Now the young men squealed and started to run! "Catch it by the tail!" cried one. "Catch it yourself!" cried another. What a racket there was! On went the kettle, rampaging round the room with its tail sticking out behind, and its badger's head sticking out in front, and the steam from the water inside lifting the lid up and down, up and down in the most uncanny way. And all the young men were squealing like pigs and throwing things at it. But no matter what, they missed it every time.

At last the young priests grew so tired of running about and throwing things that they began to make a proper plan. One of them went outside and found a rope. The others all joined hands, and very carefully they followed the kettle's movements, creeping closer and closer until they managed to drive it into a corner. Then with a shout, "Whoo-up!" one of them threw the rope and caught the kettle in a slip knot. Naturally, all the water was spilt. But the teeth went on snapping and the tail went on waggling, and it took them quite ten minutes to tie up that poor old kettle and shut it into a box.

When it was over they were simply exhausted, and even then they could not have any tea, because, of course, they had not anything to boil the water in. They all sat down feeling very sorry for themselves. Presently there came a tap at the door, and they heard the voice of a tinker crying, "Have you any old rubbish for sale? Any old knives or pails or kettles?"

Kettles! The priest and his pupils looked at one another. Very softly one of them stole tiptoe to the box and peeped in! There was the kettle lying quite quietly at the bottom of the box, and lo and behold! the tail and the head had disappeared.

One by one the priest and his pupils came up and looked at it, and all the time the old tinker was tapping at the door and crying, "Any old rubbish for sale? Any old knives, pails or kettles?"

"Come in!" said the priest. "I have got an old kettle here! Do you want to buy it? I'll sell it cheap!" All the pupils began to shiver and shake. They were terrified lest the awful tail and head should suddenly sprout again, and they did so want to get rid of the kettle, for they thought it was a hobgoblin.

The tinker, little guessing what had happened, picked up the kettle and looked at it. He undid the knots of the rope, and all the priest's pupils gibbered with fright. "It's a dusty old thing," said the tinker, "but I dare say I shall find it useful. Here you are! I can't give you more that that for it." He put three little coins into the priest's hand and walked off with the kettle under his arm. And——as he walked along, that awful tail sprouted once more, waggled "Good-bye" to the priest and his pupils, and then popped in again.

Luckily the tinker did not see it, or he might have returned the kettle and asked for his money back. Instead, he just tramped home and put the kettle in a corner among a lot of other rubbish. Then he pulled out a mat, curled himself up and went to sleep on the floor.

That night he woke up, hearing a little scratchy noise by his feet. He opened his eyes and there was the kettle which he had bought at the temple walking round the room on four furry legs! At one end

167

there was the head of a badger with teeth snip-snapping, and at the other there was a long hairy tail going wiggle-waggle, wiggle-waggle. The tinker, poor man, was in such a fright! He leapt up with a start, but no sooner was he on his feet than the kettle became a kettle again, so he lay down feeling very much puzzled.

Of course, the same thing happened night after night, until the poor tinker was quite worn out with the worry of it, for he was a kind soul. He kept thinking to himself, "If the kettle's a badger it ought to be fed! And if the badger's a kettle it ought to be boiled." He simply did not know what to do, so at last he consulted a friend. "You come and see my kettle," said he, "and then you can tell me what to do."

The friend came round that very night, and everything happened as before. The tail grew and waggled, the head of the badger snapped its teeth, and the kettle ran round on four furry legs.

"Well, you *are* silly!" said the tinker's friend, "that's a *magic* kettle! It's lucky! I'll tell you what: you be a showman. You can teach your kettle to dance and walk on a tight-rope, holding up an umbrella,

and then make people pay to come and see it. Why, you'll be rich for ever!"

And that's just exactly what happened.

It was delightful to see that little kettle dancing! Snip-snap went the teeth, wiggle-waggle went the tail. One hairy paw held up a little paper umbrella, and two hairy paws danced in the most graceful way on a tight-rope. And the whole of Japan flocked to see the wonderful kettle.

In a very few years the tinker was so rich that he retired and gave lots of money to the poor.

And finally, he gave the kettle back to the old priest and his pupils, and they made a special shelf for it and treated it with great respect. '

But it never turned into a badger again.

Why? Who knows? No doubt it was getting old, and when people get old, they like to settle down and be quiet.

King Teheser and the Nile

(Egyptian)

Long ago a river made a country. That river was the Nile and the country which it made was Egypt. By flooding the land each summer the river leaves a layer of new fertile mud in which plants can grow and animals and men live. They may not all know this story, but we know it because it was written, thousands of years ago, on a rock that was found in 1890 on the island of Sahul.

Many thousands of years ago there lived a King of Egypt whose name was Teheser. For ten years he ruled happily, rejoicing in the warm sunshine and glad that his people seemed prosperous and contented. But in the eleventh year of his reign, trouble came to Teheser. It did not come from his own subjects, nor from his enemies. It came from the River Nile, and, because of this, the trouble was greater than any that Teheser had ever known.

That year the Nile did not overflow its banks, and Teheser was frightened. He knew that the crops would fail, and men would starve if the waters of the Nile stayed where they were and did not spread over the land, making it moist and covering it with a fresh layer of fertile mud. Every year for as long as he could remember the river had overflowed, and, after a while, drawn back, leaving the land which it

had watered so rich that any seeds which were sown there flourished and increased. If the Nile had not spread itself beyond its banks, there would have been no blessing on the land, the crops would have been thin and poor, there would have been nothing for the cattle, and people would have died of starvation.

When Teheser found that the waters were not rising, he grew more and more troubled. Every morning he sent his servants down to the river to measure the height of the water on the banks, and every evening they returned with the same story: "Oh, great pharaoh, the waters of the Nile are still. The river has not left its banks."

At first Teheser's subjects did not complain. They were sorry that the river had failed them, but they knew that the King's barns were full of grain from the last year's harvest, and they hoped that in the coming year the Nile would bring them richer soil than ever before. But the next year the same thing happened. The earth was parched and dry. The river scarcely seemed to move. There was no overflow of water, and the seeds which were sown in the thirsty ground found no nourishment and had hardly strength enough to show their green blades above the earth.

For five years the river failed to bless the land. Teheser sat miserably in his palace wondering what to do. There was no grain in the barns. There were no grapes in the vineyards. Even the dates and figs were dry, and the wretched cattle could scarcely stand. The mules which had once drawn Teheser's chariot through the streets were now so thin and weak that the pharaoh was obliged to walk lest they should fall beneath his weight.

His walks through the city made Teheser weep for sorrow. Everywhere men, women and children were dying of hunger. Their bodies were gaunt and thin, their eyes wild. Their hearts were growing hard, and sometimes, when they saw one of their neighbours with a scrap of meat or a fig, they would seize the morsel and eat it themselves.

Teheser went into the temples and prayed. He consulted many priests, and he said a prayer in each place, for in those days the Egyptians worshipped many different gods, each of whom had his own temple. But the gods made no answer to Teheser, and still the Nile spread no blessing beyond its banks.

Then Teheser sent for all his wise men and his governors. One by one they came into his palace and bowed before his throne. They were so thin and hungry that their eyes had sunk far into their heads, and Teheser could see the bones under their skin.

"Has pharaoh need of us?" they asked.

"Hear me!" said Teheser. "I have said many prayers. I have knelt in the temples with my forehead in the dust. I have put ashes on my head. I have begged the gods to spread out the waters of the Nile that my fields may be fruitful. But not one has made an answer to my prayer, and now my people starve. You are the wisest of my men, who help me to govern. Speak and tell me what I should do to help my hungry country."

For a short time there was silence. Then an old man came slowly up the hall, and, kneeling before Teheser, spoke. His voice was weak. "Hear me, great pharaoh," he whispered, "for I come from the south and I know where the Nile has its source. It is to the God of the Nile that you must pray."

Teheser listened, bending forward to hear the hoarse whisper.

173

"Hear me, great pharaoh!" murmured the old man. "In the region which I rule in your name lies the island of Elephantine. There is a cavern on this island. It is deep, and within it, far below the earth, are the waters which make the Nile, kept back by a rocky door. Khnemu, the God of the Nile, watches over them. When the time comes for the river to overflow its banks, he draws aside the bolts, the door opens and the water gushes out and blesses the land."

Teheser sighed. "For five years Khnemu has not drawn the bolts," he said.

The old man nodded. "Hear me again, great pharaoh," he answered. "Khnemu sits in the Temple of the Gods at Elephantine, motionless as rock. Year after year he has sent good gifts to the men of Egypt, but no one has remembered his name. No one has sent him a thank-offering of corn or fruit." Tears fell from the old man's eyes. "Shall Khnemu bless the land which forgets him?" he asked.

Sorrowful and ashamed, Teheser left the hall, and although he was hungry and weary with the great heat of the sun, he left the palace and never rested until he had reached the island of Elephantine.

He made his way to the Temple of the Gods, and because he had neither fruit nor corn, he laid his jewels as an offering to Khnemu. Kneeling, with his forehead touching the ground, he prayed to Khnemu, begging him to save the people of Egypt and once again unbar the door that the waters might rush out and bless the land. The words of his prayer showed all the sorrow that was in his heart and the great love that he had for his people.

As he lay on the ground he seemed to feel a hand touching his head, and to hear a voice which said, "I am Khnemu. I am the Nile which rises to give a blessing to all who toil upon the earth. I am Khnemu, the father of the gods. I am Khnemu, whom men have forgotten. My shrine is broken and no one has rebuilt it. I bless the land with fruitfulness, yet no man has brought me fruit. Teheser at last has remembered me, and I will have pity on his misery. Go back, pharaoh, and bid your people remember Khnemu, who will unbolt the door every year so that the Nile may rise once again and bring a blessing to the land."

Tears of joy stood in Teheser's eyes, and he looked up and cried, "Oh, great Khnemu, God of the Nile, giver of blessings, who sends bread to my starving people, never again shall your name be forgotten."

He rose from his knees, bowed low and left the temple.

The next day the waters of the Nile began to rise and overflow their banks, and in every town and village Teheser's subjects listened to his royal commands. Land on either side of the Nile was to be kept for the temple of Khnemu. Priests were to serve him, and never again was his shrine to fall into disrepair.

As the people watched the water overflowing the river's banks and heard the proclamation, they stretched out their hands towards the Nile and cried, "Blessed be Khnemu!"

The Man who Married a Fairy

(*Celtic*)

This story is borrowed from someone called Walter Map who included it in his book, *De Nugis Curialium* or *Courtiers' Trifles*. He wrote it 800 years ago in Latin in a dark little stone room in a castle on the Welsh border. He believed in all sorts of queer things, such as demons and fairy women, and he wrote about them quite seriously, as though they were real.

There was once a man who lived on the edge of a forest. He was all alone. He could only get meat by hunting the wild animals which roamed through the woods, and he could only get bread by grinding the corn, which grew in a little patch of ground not far from his cottage. A cow gave him milk, and his own bees gave him honey, and if he wanted water, he carried a pail to the edge of the wood and dipped it into the running brook.

Of course he was lonely. When he went to his bee-hive and saw all the bees humming loudly, he used to think, "Ah! even the bees have friends, and don't live all alone. I wish I had a little wife, with eyes as brown as the body of a bee." When he went into his field and saw the ears of corn clustered close together, he used to sigh and say, "Look at the corn. Even that doesn't live alone. I wish I had a little wife with hair as yellow as corn." When he went to the brook to draw water, and saw how the fallen leaves played on its surface, and how the brook chattered and laughed as it passed over the pebbles, he used

to say, "Even the brook talks to its neighbours. I *wish* I had a little wife with a laugh that rippled like the water passing over the stones."

It was strange! Nothing in the world seemed to be lonely except himself.

One night he felt sadder than ever. He didn't quite know why. It could have been the fault of the birds. You see the man slept very close under the roof, and at night he used to hear the birds chattering to one another in the eaves. That particular night they seemed to be very excited, and they were chirping and twittering so much that the man could not sleep. He got up and went outside, and sat down on the step, saying, "If only I had a little wife who'd go about the house singing like a little bird."

Then, because he was so lonely and did not want to think about himself any more, he jumped up and strode away into the darkness.

It was a queer grey night, and the moon was not up, though he could just see a tiny rim of silver. The clouds were scudding across the sky, and whenever the man's footsteps made the slightest sound, the wind in the trees whispered, "*Hussssh!*" and the startled owls peered down on him and asked, "*Whoo*-are you? *Whooo*-are you?"

He took no notice, but strode straight on, and presently the moon floated up from behind the lake and made a silver path across it. The man sat down and looked across the water. He was thinking, "If I had a wife I would give her a silver ribbon for her hair, as silver as the pathway of the moon."

As he was thinking, the moon seemed to shine more brightly than ever. The bulrushes which grew round the lake swayed and whispered. "*Hussssh!*" said the trees, and there came a sound like the wind passing through a forest, like the tinkling of hare-bells in the wood.

A shadow passed over the lake, and the waters were ruffled, and suddenly hundreds of bubbles rose to the surface and burst. The man watched. He seemed to hear voices. Slowly, like a soft grey mist coming up from the water, shadowy figures arose, and the man saw that there were women. Their hair floated out behind them, and they came dancing towards him, waving their white arms, and singing with voices as sweet and clear as a blackbird's.

The man gazed and gazed, but they passed him by as though they had not seen him, and then—he noticed something. He saw that one of the ladies was more beautiful than any of the others. Her golden hair was finer, her red lips were rosier, her white arms were whiter. There was a broad silver ribbon round her head. She sang like a bird, her laughter was like a ripple of water over shining pebbles, her hair was like corn, and her eyes were as brown as the body of a bee.

The lovely ladies danced till the sun stole up from behind the hills. Then the wind said *"Husssh!"*, the bulrushes whispered, the dancers drifted across the water and disappeared into the lake.

The man went home. He did not feel lonely, for he dreamt until late in the morning of the fairy lady of the lake. The next night he went out again and waited by the water, while the trees whispered *"Husssh,"* and the owls said, *"Whooo* are yooou?" All happened as before. The moon shone brightly, hundreds of bubbles arose, and out of the lake came the fairy women. They danced like flowers in the spring. They sang like birds in the early morning, and they came floating past the man at the water's edge like thistledown drifting in a breeze. The man stretched out his hand and touched the most beautiful of all the dancers. She laughed, and the sound was like the water of a brook trickling through the woods. But he could not stop her. She floated up into the air, whirled like an autumn leaf in the wind, and disappeared with her sisters into the lake.

The man went home, and again he dreamed about the fairy lady. The next night be returned to the lake, but this time he hid in a different place, behind a rock near the edge of the water. The moon was very bright, and the silver path across the lake was more dazzling than ever. The trees were quite still, but the bulrushes whispered, "He's there! He's there!" The man crouched lower and waited.

Again all happened as before. Out of the lake rose the fairy dancers. Their little white feet twinkled like stars, their golden hair floated behind them like clouds in a sunset. They drifted across the water, and when they came to the sand at the edge of the lake, they whirled and circled and swayed, dancing and singing as though nothing would stop them. The most beautiful of all danced towards the rock singing, "Follow me! Follow me, sisters!" She sped across the sand, and the man put out both his arms and caught her. He felt her breath. It fluttered against his cheek like a butterfly, but she was cold, as cold as the mist which rose from the lake. Then all the bulrushes swayed and struggled, and the branches of the trees whispered, "He's caught a fairy!" A cloud hit the face of the moon. Calling, "Lost! Lost! Lost!" the other dancers sank beneath the water.

The man went home with the fairy in his arms. He saw that her hair was as gold as corn and her eyes as brown as a bee's body. He took her into his cottage and put her into a chair, and warmed some milk for her to drink, and gave her a little oaten cake, but she would not eat anything, and for three days she never spoke. Then she said, "Good morning, husband! I will be a good wife to you. I will sweep your house and cook your meals and plant seeds in your garden. I will do everything for you until the day when you scold me and speak angrily of my sisters."

The man smiled and said, "That will never happen." He was very happy with his fairy wife. She sang about the house like a bird, and when she laughed the sound was like water rippling over pebbles. The man was happy because he was no longer lonely.

One day, after they had been married for several years, he wanted to go hunting. He had seen the tracks of a wolf in the forest; they were fresh tracks, and he wished to go quickly. "Wife," he cried, "little wife! Bring me cake and wine quickly, for I'm going out hunting." But his wife did not come. She was upstairs combing her hair and singing a song. "Wife," he cried again, and "Wife! *Wife!* WIFE!" and she came strolling out, laughing, to see what he wanted.

His face was black with rage. "Why are you so slow?" he scolded. "I bade you hasten. I suppose you were kept by those dancing sisters of yours! Bring me wine and cake. Hurry!" and he pushed her angrily. And——and she vanished.

Flip——just like that. At one minute he scolded her, and the next minute she was not there. He was frightened. "Wife," he cried, "little wife! Where are you?" But nobody answered. He only heard the trees say, "*Husssh!*" He only felt a cold wind blow past his face, and he saw a little grey cloud float towards the lake and disappear into the water.

Ever afterwards he was a lonely old man. He used to go back to the lake and wait and wait for the fairy women, but they never came again. Never once did he see a golden-haired dancer with eyes as brown as the body of a bee, with the voice of a bird, and laughter which rippled like water trickling over the stones. Sometimes he cried, "Oh, dear little wife, what made you go?" And only the wind answered, "*Yooou*-You."

Monacella and her Little Lambs

(Welsh)

Monacella is the patron saint of hares. She is also called St. Melangell, and the day which is sacred to her is May 27th. She founded a church in Montgomeryshire.

The lord of the land in the story was really the Prince of Powys. He is supposed to have found Monacella with the hare nestling against her dress in the year 604. He gave her some land, and for hundreds of years people used to call the hares "Wyn Melangell", or "Monacella's lambs". Nobody would kill a hare in the parish. If they saw one being hunted, they used to shout, "God and Monacella be with thee," and it was sure to escape.

There are many beautiful legends about saints and animals. There was St. Jerome who made friends with a lion who used to watch over him and St. Andrew, who once preached to the fish, and they put their heads out of the water to hear what he had to say, and St. Columba, who read the Bible to a donkey which had strayed into the chapel, when nobody else had come to the service.

And, greatest of all, the story of St. Francis, who preached to the birds, who all stopped singing to listen to him. He once talked to a fierce wolf which had terrorised the villagers until it became so gentle that everyone grew to love it, and grieved when at last it died.

There was once a princess who lived among the mountains of Wales. Her name was Monacella, and everyone loved her because she was so kind and gentle. If the village people were ill, Monacella would go and sit with them, nursing them, telling them stories, and bringing them warm nourishing soups. If she met a child crying, Monacella

would dry its tears and comfort it. If she met a poor little animal which was hurt, she took it to the castle, bound up its wounds, fed it until it was well, and then carried it back to the woods and let it run away home.

When Monacella was sixteen she was so beautiful and so famous for her gentleness, that princes came to her father's castle, asking to marry her. One of the princes was very grand. He had a large castle and many soldiers to fight for him, and when Monacella's father saw him he thought, "Ah! my daughter shall marry this prince. He's so powerful that he will help me to fight against all my enemies. With his help I shall be able to burn castles and carry off prisoners and booty!" So he sent for Monacella and said, "Daughter, call your sewing maids to sew and embroider for you. You must have some beautiful clothes, for you are going to marry a great prince, who will help me to fight against my enemies!"

But Monacella was very unhappy. She did not care a bit about beautiful clothes, and she did not want to marry a prince. She hated life in the castle, where people were always fighting and burning, killing and carrying off prisoners. She did not want to marry and live in another castle where her husband would be doing exactly the same things as her father.

So she went up to her little room in the tower and she sat down and thought. She said to herself, "I don't want to live here. I don't want to live in another prince's castle. I want to go to a place where there will be no more war and fighting and cruelty—a lovely quiet place where I can pray to God and live in peace."

That night Monacella packed a little basket of food, crept out of her father's castle and went away into the woods. For a long time she wandered about, climbing the hills and passing through the forests, until she came to a copse in a beautiful green valley.

Monacella sat down to rest, and she looked about her. At her feet rippled a little stream, and not far away she saw two overhanging rocks which formed a sort of cave. When Monacella saw the cave she was delighted. She knelt down on the grass and lifted her face to the sky, saying, "Thank you, God, for sending me a little home."

Then she stood up and began to gather moss and bracken, and when she had collected enough she made herself a bed in the cave. She felt very happy, for she knew that she was going to be quite quiet and peaceful.

For a long time Monacella was alone in her little copse. She drank from the stream and she fed upon wild berries. But by and by the people from the valley found out that she was there, and they came to make friends with her. After that, Monacella used to go to their

187

houses and nurse their sick and look after their babies. The people
of the valley grew to love her very dearly because she was so gentle
and holy. They used to bring her fruit from their gardens, fresh eggs,
and little cakes, so that she need no longer drink only water and eat
only berries.

But there were others who learned to love Monacella besides the
people of the valley. These were the woodland folk. The thrushes and
the blackbirds loved her, and when she sang her morning hymn, they
sang too. The little brown wrens, the robins, sparrows and starlings
all learned to love her. And when she peeped into their nests to look
at their babies or their pretty little speckled eggs, they were none of
them afraid. The weasels, the foxes and the badgers, the hedgehogs,
the rabbits and the hares popped out from the bracken when she came
past, and said, "Good-day, Monacella! God bless you!" And she
answered, "God bless all the beasts of the wood."

One morning, long after Monacella had left her father's castle, a
little brown hare went loping through the valley. The sun was shining,
and he felt very comfortable, so he did not hurry. He stopped to nibble
the grass. Whenever he found a juicy bud or a tender root, he wrinkled
up his nose and wobbled his little stumpy tail, and whispered, "Ooooh,
delicious!"

He was really enjoying himself when suddenly he heard a sound which made his ears twitch with fear and his eyes grow big and frightened. He turned first this way and then that, and he sniffed the air. Down the breeze came the sound of a horn and the distant barking of dogs. The lord of the land was hunting, and his hounds had picked up the scent of the little hare.

"Oh, dear! Oh, dear!" thought the hare. "I must run. I must run like the wind." And away he scampered through the green valley, in and out among the thickets and brambles, past the marshes and up the hills, and all the time he was saying to himself, "I want Monacella! If I can find Monacella I shall be safe."

He twisted and turned and he doubled back, but the young lord's hounds were the fastest in the land, and on they came, twenty hounds to one poor little hare.

"Ho-ho! Ho-ho! We must catch that hare!" bayed the hounds, and "I must get to Monacella! I must get to Monacella!" cried the hare, and darted through the bushes and over the mosses and dead leaves into Monacella's little wood, with the hounds coming helter-skelter behind—so close, so terribly close, that they nearly snapped at the little hare's brown fur.

Oh, what a scuttering, scurrying and rushing! What a crackling of

leaves and pattering of feet! The hounds were in full cry, the little hare running, and all the birds and the beasts and even the wind were whispering, "Monacella! Monacella! Someone's in trouble! Where are you?"

Then there was a little rustle among the grasses, and a clear voice said, "God bless all the beasts in the wood!"

Suddenly everything was quite quiet.

Down in the valley came the faint sound of a horn, and in a few minutes the lord of the land came riding up to the wood. He had to part the branches to get through, but he knew he was right. He knew that his hounds had driven a little hare into this wood.

"Here! Here! Dogs!" he called, but his hounds did not answer, and the wood was very still. The young lord called again, and pushed his way through a thicket into a little open space.

He stopped with astonishment. There on a rock, with her eyes closed and her hands folded, sat a beautiful lady in a grey robe. At her feet was a little brown hare, and sitting in a circle looking up at her were all his own hounds!

When they saw their master coming, the hounds looked round and their tails went thump, thump, thump on the ground, and their big brown eyes seemed to say, "We don't know what's happened! But we can't do anything while she's saying her prayers."

And, strange to say, when the lord of the land saw Monacella, he was just like the hounds. He did not want to kill or to hunt, and he suddenly felt very glad that the little brown hare was safe.

When Monacella opened her eyes, the young man's face was very red and his voice a little husky. "Lady," he said, "I don't know who you are, but I know you're gentle and kind. God sent this little hare to you for safety." Then he took off his silk cap and he bowed very low. "Because you are gentle and love the wild things, I will give you this valley. It shall be a sanctuary. Nobody shall ever again hunt hares or set traps so long as the beasts of the wood live near you."

He called his dogs, and one by one they licked Monacella's hand and went away. And all the time the little hare sat on her robe and did not look the tiniest bit frightened.

After that nobody ever hunted in that part of the valley, and Monacella lived there in peace. And all the hares from near at hand came to live with her. They scampered in front when she walked, they peeped from behind the bushes when she prayed. Wherever she went they pattered about with her.

When the shepherds in the valley were driving their sheep home to the folds, they sometimes met Monacella with the hares scampering at her feet, and they used to smile and say, "There goes the shepherdess with her lambs! Goodnight, Monacella! God bless all the beasts of the wood."

Sonia
and the Twelve Months

(Russian)

This story in one variation or another is one of the most widely known *skazki* or fairy-tales of Russia. Instead of the Twelve Months it may be the Four Seasons that Sonia finds and King December may be Grandfather Frost—a character who in many ways resembles our Father Christmas or Santa Claus. He is an important figure in the Russian New Year festivities presiding over parties and providing the children with sweets and toys.

You will notice that the story talks about Natasha and Sonia sleeping *on* the stove and on this page you will see children doing so. This stove, or *petch* as it is called, serves many purposes in a Russian cottage. It is actually a large baking oven heated by a log fire which burns inside it. While the fire is burning cooking is done above and fish is smoked in the chimney, which is in front. Then, when the fire dies down, the ashes are swept out and baking is done. After that it is used as a steam bath, for it is just large enough for a man to crouch in. Finally, as we have seen, the whole family climbs up two or three steps and sleeps on the platform above-and behind the chimney and so keeps warm through the very cold winter nights.

Once upon a time there was a little girl called Sonia, who lived in a cottage in the middle of a deep forest in the heart of Russia. Sonia did not wear the sort of clothes that are worn in other countries, but she had very pretty things. Instead of a hat she wore a red handkerchief tied over her hair and under her chin. She wore a white linen blouse with very wide sleeves and the shoulders and collar and cuffs embroidered in a pattern of red and black. She had also a scarlet apron, which she did not wear round her waist, but tied high up underneath her armpits. If she was cold she put on a coat made of sheepskin, and boots of felt which came up to her knees.

Sonia had no mother, yet she was quite happy because she loved her father very much. But one day something happened which changed her life altogether. Her father married again, and the stepmother brought to the house a big girl of her own. This girl was called Natasha, and instead of being a good sister to Sonia, she was very unkind to her. From the first minute that she arrived in the cottage she began to torment the poor child.

"Dear me," she said, when she saw four places laid at the table. "Why is there an extra place here? Clear it away at once!"

"But that's Sonia's place," said her old father.

"Oh, indeed!" said Natasha, "and who's going to wait at the table, I should like to know? Clear away that place! Now, Sonia, hand round the plates."

So poor little Sonia had to hand round the plates and dishes, and had nothing to eat until everybody else had finished, and usually there was very little left.

She was very sad. She wondered whether that would happen every night, and she felt quite afraid to go to bed because she knew that she would have to sleep next to Natasha. She crept very softly up to the big square stove on top of which Natasha was sleeping, rolled in a blanket. But Natasha would not make room for Sonia, and so poor Sonia had to lie on the floor.

After that she always lay on the floor and she always waited at table. In fact, she cooked all the meals and did all the housework, and was always being scolded from morning till night. Her father felt he could not do anything to help her. If he said anything in her favour, his wife and his stepdaughter made everything so uncomfortable for him that he was afraid to speak. And so he left poor Sonia alone, and she became nothing better than a little slave.

Of course, she was very tired and very unhappy, but somehow or other she never looked cross, and she grew prettier and prettier every day. Natasha had pretty hair and pretty eyes and a pretty little nose and a pretty little mouth, but she always looked so bad-tempered that she

194

did not look pretty. Whenever Natasha looked at her own face in the glass and then looked at Sonia's, she felt very jealous, and she longed to get rid of Sonia.

She thought and thought and thought, and at last she made a plan.

One cold winter's morning, when the snow was lying on the ground and long blue icicles hung from the roof, she called, "Sonia, put down that needlework and go and get me some violets."

"Violets!" said Sonia. "Why, Natasha, we're in the middle of winter! How can I find violets?"

"Winter or not," said Natasha, "I want violets and I'm going to have them, and, what is more, you are going to get them. Out you go.

If you come back without the violets, I shall lock the door and the wolves of the forest will come and eat you up."

"Dear, *dear* Natasha," said Sonia, "how can I get violets when the snow covers everything?"

"*I* don't know," said Natasha, "but violets I intend to have. Out you go!" and she took up a broom and drove Sonia out of the house without even giving her time to put on her sheepskin coat.

It was a very cold day! Feathery flakes of snow were falling fast. You could not see a patch of earth on the ground, it was so white. The snow lay a foot high on the branches of the trees. Poor little Sonia slid and stumbled through the forest, looking everywhere for a little patch of bare ground where she might find some violets.

On and on she went. Presently the sky grew dark, and the snow fell faster, and she could hear the wolves barking in the distance, and she grew very frightened and longed for the warm stove in the little cottage, but she was afraid to go back without the violets. So she went on and on through the dark forest.

Just as she was beginning to feel so tired that she wanted to lie down in the snow, she saw a little light in the distance.

"A cottage!" she thought. "Oh, perhaps they'll let me go in and rest and warm myself." And she began to run as fast as her tired limbs would carry her.

As she ran, the light seemed to grow brighter and bigger until it cast a rosy glow all over the snow, and Sonia saw that it was not the light from a cottage, but a big fire round which twelve people were sitting.

They were men. The oldest was on a throne and he held a sceptre in his hand. He was so old that his hair looked like snow, his eyes were blue and glassy as icicles, and his beard was so long that it touched the ground and seemed like the thin twigs of a tree covered with hoar frost. "Maiden," he said, "what do you want in the land of the Twelve Months? I am King December; why have you come to disturb me?"

"Oh, sir," said Sonia. "I am sorry if I have disturbed you. I only want to warm my hands at your fire, for I'm very cold and I've come a long way."

Then the eleven men moved aside, and Sonia stood by King December and warmed her hands at the fire. She tried to keep back her tears, but one by one they rolled down her cheeks and fell on December's robes—and as they did so she saw that they turned into little glassy beads of ice.

"Maiden," said December, "why are you unhappy?" Then Sonia told him how she had been sent out to fetch violets and how her step-sister was going to let the wolves eat her if she came home without them.

When December heard this he stood up and moved away from the throne. "March," said he, "take my sceptre," and a young man with

wavy hair and clear blue eyes took the sceptre from December and sat on the throne. As he did so, he waved his hand. The snow began to melt, a tree which was stiff with frost burst into green buds, and the air seemed full of the scents of spring. Sonia looked down at her feet.

There she saw green moss and a host of nodding violets.

"Gather them quickly," said March, "for I cannot sit here for long."

Crying, "Oh thank you, thank you!" Sonia stooped and began to pick the violets. As soon as she had gathered a handful, March gave the sceptre back to December and helped him on to the throne. Then the snow and the ice returned, and once again winter reigned. But Sonia had her violets. She thanked the Months and ran so quickly through the forest that she reached the cottage before the doors were locked for the night.

Natasha and her stepmother were astonished and amazed when they saw the violets. They could scarcely believe their eyes. They tried to make Sonia tell them how she found the flowers, but all that she said was, "I gathered them in the forest."

The next day Natasha consulted with her mother. "Let's make her find a basket full of strawberries this time," she said. "She'll never manage *that* in the middle of winter. If she doesn't bring them back, we'll lock the doors and let the wolves eat her. How I hate her pretty face!"

"Yes," said her mother, "that's a good idea! Come here, Sonia! Go out into the forest and fill this basket with strawberries. If you don't bring back some sweet fresh ones, we'll lock the doors and the wolves shall eat you." She took up a broom and drove Sonia out of the cottage.

Sonia ran through the forest crying, "Oh where can I find the Twelve Months? If *only* I could find the Twelve Months!"

For hours she wandered through the snow, and once again just as she was longing to go to sleep she saw the glow of a fire, and there was dear old December sitting on his throne with the eleven months around him.

"What is it this time?" asked December.

"Strawberries!" wept Sonia, and once again her tears fell like glass beads on his foot.

Then December rose from his throne, and as he did so flakes of snow dropped from his hair and his breath was like an icy wind. "Take my sceptre, June," he said—and a young man with golden hair and blue eyes took the sceptre and sat on the throne. Immediately the snow melted, and among the leaves at her feet Sonia saw hundreds of scarlet strawberries.

"Gather them quickly, Sonia," said June, "for I can't stay in December's place for long."

Then Sonia filled her basket, and when she had gathered the last strawberry, December returned to the throne and once again the forest was white with snow.

"Go home, little Sonia," said the Twelve Months, and before she knew what had happened, Sonia found herself at the cottage door.

"Here are your strawberries," she said, and Natasha and her mother could hardly speak for astonishment. But they ate all the strawberries and did not give Sonia one.

"Where did you get them?"

"I gathered them in the forest!" said Sonia.

"Then," said Natasha, "to-morrow *I* shall go and find some."

She was as good as her word. The very next day she wrapped herself

in a fur coat, put on felt boots and a warm fur cap, and set out to look
for violets and strawberries in the snow.

On and on she tramped, getting crosser every minute because the
snow was so deep. At last she saw the light of the fire, and there was
old December still on the throne and the other Months sitting around
him. Natasha pushed her way towards the fire and began to warm her
hands.

"Maiden," said the Months, "what do you want?"

"Mind your own business!" said Natasha, and began to poke about
in the snow, looking for strawberries and violets.

Then, quite suddenly, *the fire flickered and went out*.

December touched Natasha with his cold, cold fingers and whispered
something in her ear. His breath was like the coldest blast. It made

Natasha so stiff that she fell to the ground. December shook his head, and snowflakes fluttered down and covered her till nothing could be seen but the tip of her little fur cap.

Of course, she never came home. Her mother waited and waited and then went out to look for her, and she, too, never came home. Both mother and daughter had disappeared. Sonia never knew what had happened to them. Sometimes she thought she heard them crying outside, but when she opened the door, she only felt the wind. Natasha and her mother had vanished.

As for Sonia, a nice prince came and carried her off, and they were married on a winter's day, and everyone wondered where they had found the violets which decorated the church and the delicious strawberries which were served at the feast.

The Luck of
Ianto Llewelyn

(Welsh)

Remembering how fairy stories have grown and developed over the many years they have been travelling around the world, it is quite possible that this story was once the same story as *The Mannikins and the Green Peas,* but changed in the course of its journey from Wales to Germany or perhaps from Germany to Wales.

This is a fairy story. Many people don't believe in fairies, but this story is about someone who did; and the queer thing about "believing" is that if you believe them hard enough, the oddest things can seem to be true. Ianto Llewelyn believed in fairies, and so, of course, they came to live in his house.

His house was an odd one—and somehow quite uncomfortable. It was not even made of bricks and mortar; it was made of sticks and branches, stuck together with mud and thatched with straw. The floor was just bare earth, with little bits of grass peeping up between the stones.

And as for the door, it did not fit! There was a crack down the middle and a space between it and the floor, and when it was cold, the wind would come howling round the hut, creep under the door and try to blow out Ianto's fire. And Ianto had to stuff the space under the door with hay. He could not allow the fire to be blown out, for what would the fairies have done if he had? They are shivery little folk who like to keep warm. Ianto knew this, and, sure enough, when he went to bed, he always left the fire burning. He often heard them pattering about the room at night, and when the fire crackled and burnt up with a quick, bright spurt, he knew that they were warming their hands and toes, and he used to chuckle to himself and call out, "Good luck to you, little people. Put on a bit more wood if you want it. Make yourselves at home."

Then he would curl himself under a blanket and sleep soundly. He never once looked at the fairies, because he was really fond of them, and if one is fond of a person, one tries to do what that person likes, and not to do what he does not like. Ianto knew that the fairies liked to be warm, and that they did *not* like to be seen. And, what is more, he knew that if one talked about them or mentioned them by name, they would go away and never come back, and of course he did not want that to happen; so Ianto Llewelyn was most careful not to look for the fairies and never to mention them to anybody.

One cold night, when Ianto had made up a bigger fire than usual and gone to bed with the blankets tucked well round his shoulders, the firelight spurted up, and he heard the little people drawing closely round the flames and talking.

"Ee," said one in a high, squeaky voice, "it's cold and I'm hungry. I'd like some bread and cheese."

"Uum," said another, "so'd I! Ianto Llewelyn has a bit of bread and cheese in the cupboard. Let's take it."

There was a minute's silence, and then Ianto heard a little scuffle and an angry voice saying, "Pinch him! Pull his ears! Tug his hair!

The greedy little thing!" and a frightened voice cried, "Ee, ee, ee! Let me go! You hurt!"

"Then don't say that again!" said the angry voice. "Take Ianto Llewelyn's bread and cheese, indeed! Why, he's very poor. He's only got a morsel and that's for his breakfast."

When Ianto heard that, he popped up his head and said, "Hey! little people, take what you want and welcome. I wish you good appetite." Then he tucked the blanket round his head again and went to sleep without giving so much as half a glance at the fairies.

The next morning he got up and straightened the house, and was just going to lay the table when he remembered that he had given his bread and cheese to the fairies. "Heigh-ho," said he. "Well, I must just go hungry, that's all." So he tightened his belt and went to the cupboard to get a cup for a drink of water. And—imagine his surprise— on the shelf was a large loaf of bread, a pat of butter and a piece of fresh cheese.

He knew where they came from! The fairies, of course. No sooner did Ianto see this gift than he waved in the direction of the woods

and said, "Thank you kindly, little people; good luck to you. May you never be penniless!"

Just as he said that—"whit!"—something shot through the air, and there on the hob beside the kettle was a bright new silver shilling. "Goodness gracious me!" said Ianto, and picked it up. No sooner had he done so than—"whit!"—there was another one on the hob. "My eye and Betty Martin!" said Ianto, and picked that up too. "Whit!"—something else whizzed through the air and lo and behold! another shilling lay shining on the hob.

The same thing happened time after time. And at last Ianto had so many shillings that his pocket was quite heavy, and still another lay on the hob.

Once again he knew where they had come from! The fairies, of course. "Thank you kindly, little people," said Ianto, waving in the direction of the woods. "Good luck to you indeed," and he put on his hat and went down the hill into the town, singing and laughing to himself, for he knew that he was a rich man.

The first thing he did was to buy himself a little cottage, with honeysuckle climbing up the door and an apple tree in front and a patch of potatoes behind. And he left the cold little hut with the badly

fitting door and went to live in the new cottage. But he was very, very careful to keep the fire burning all night so that the fairies came, too.

Naturally, with a new shilling coming—"whit"—through the air whenever he picked the old one off the hob, Ianto soon became a rich man. He bought a cart and horse, two cows, and a very handsome pig. He bought a few chickens and a cat to sit on the mat and lick her paws in front of the fire; and he had new blankets for the bed and a pair of good corduroy breeches so that he could throw away the old ones which had a patch behind. When he was really well set up he went a-courting and brought home a bride.

Now sometimes this is a mistake, but men *will* do it—and Ianto was just like everybody else. He wanted to settle down, and now that he had a new house and plenty of money to buy good food, he wanted a wife to keep the place tidy and cook his meals.

And if she *had* done that, it would have been all right. But the very first thing she did when she crossed the threshold was to say, "Oh, Ianto, you careless boy! You've left a shilling on the hob. Fancy, if a thief came in! There—put it in your pocket and don't leave it about again."

She picked it up and—whit!—something whizzed through the window, and there was another shilling. The little bride rubbed her eyes. She looked at the shilling in her hand, and she looked at the shilling on the hob. Then she stretched out her hand and was going to pick up the second shilling when Ianto took her by the wrist.

"That's the luck of the house," he said, and he gave her a kiss.

"Where does it come from?" she asked.

"Now don't you talk so much," said Ianto. "Come and have supper."

They sat down to supper, but the new bride kept looking at the hob.

"Oh, Ianto," she said. "I'm your wife and you won't tell me where the shilling comes from. I do think you're unkind."

"Whist, now! Be quiet!" said Ianto. "I tell you it's the luck of the house."

"I know it's the luck of the house, but how did it get there? Shillings don't always come—whit!—through—"

"Oh, don't they!" said Ianto, "but they do *here*! Now that's enough!

Get on with your supper. And look here, before we go to bed to-night, mind you make up a big fire."

"Ianto! How can you ask such a thing? Why, we might be burnt in our beds—and, anyhow, it's a wicked waste."

"Now, now, now!" said Ianto, beginning to get cross. "Don't argue! If you want a shilling to be there in the morning, you must make up a fire at night. Do you hear what I say?"

"Why, Ianto," cried the little bride, "I do believe you think it's the fair—."

"Sssh!"

The next day, and for several days, Ianto's wife busied herself about the house. When she wanted to go shopping she took a shilling off the hob—and whit!—another flew through the window and took its place.

It was very pleasant, and the bride was glad to have so much money, but she longed to know where it came from, and day and night, she teased Ianto with her questions, now coaxing, now crying, now sulking, now stamping her foot, now saying, "You don't really love me if you won't tell me," until the poor fellow did not know whether he was on his head or his heels.

One morning after they had been married for a fortnight, Ianto took seven silver shillings off the hob and went out. But his wife followed him into the garden, saying, "Oh, do tell! Oh, Ianto, darling, *is* it the fairies?"

And suddenly Ianto lost his patience. "Yes!" he cried. "It *is* the fairies. Go home and don't bother me any more."

Neither of them heard the patter of little feet. Neither of them heard the squeak of angry voices, but they both felt a cold wind. And when Ianto put his hand in his pocket to take the seven shillings, he drew out seven dead leaves.

He had forgotten! He had spoken of the fairies by name, and the

luck of the house was gone. He was poor after that. There were no more shillings on the hob. Only dead leaves blew through the window. Ianto and his wife had to leave the new cottage and go and live in the old mud hut, and although they kept the fire burning every night the little folk never came back.

And the queer thing was that Ianto stopped believing in them after that, and when you no longer believe in a thing, naturally, you never see it again.

Prince Beppo and the Oranges

(Italian)

The oranges we have today have travelled even farther than the magic ones in this story. The first trees grew in the far east of Asia. Then gradually gardeners farther and farther to the west planted and tended them—in Asia Minor, the Mediterranean lands, Africa, America and finally Australia. Now the orange has travelled round the world and is at home in many countries.

Once upon a time there was a prince called Beppo who wished to get married. He wanted a bride with hair as golden as orange peel, with skin as white as an orange blossom, and a temper as sweet as orange juice. But he could not find one! No, there wasn't a girl like that in the whole city. So the prince set out to seek his fortune.

He put on old clothes and he took a staff in his hand, and he went out in the early hours of the morning when everyone was asleep and the sun was only just beginning to rise.

He had never been by himself before, and he felt very happy because he had time to look about him and notice things. He noticed the dandelions and the daisies by the wayside. He noticed the many different notes of the birds, and he noticed the dew on the grass and

the sunbeams in the hedge. And then he noticed something quite unexpected. It was a leg! Yes, somebody's brown, hairy, bony leg sticking out from under the hedge. Then he noticed something else. This time he did not see it. He heard it! It was a groan like this. "Ah-aaaah!"

"Good gracious!" exclaimed the prince. "Wait a minute. I'll help you." And he seized the leg and pulled. Hurrupp! *And*—out came a beggar—such a poor ragged old thing, with such a straggling beard and such a *scratched* face. He really was a miserable object.

"Good gracious!" exclaimed the prince again. "You poor old man. You don't look as though you've had anything to eat for a week. Here, take this bag of food. Now, here's some money, put that in your pocket. And now I'm going to give

you my cloak. You'll be quite warm." He wrapped his cloak round the poor old man, and was just about to go away when the beggar cried, "Stop! Where are you off to?" "Me?" asked the prince. "Why, I'm going to look for a bride with hair as gold as orange peel, with skin as white as an orange blossom, and a temper as sweet as orange juice." "Hm!" said the old beggar, "you don't say so! Well, you'll meet three witches first! they've got one oven where they bake their bread, but they've nothing to clean it with! They have to use their hands. You give them a bunch of twigs and they'll let you pass."

"Thank you very much," said the prince. "I won't forget. Goodbye!" And he picked a bunch of twigs from the nearest tree and went off.

He had not gone very far before the country began to change. Very soon there was no grass and there were no trees. The prince walked on, looking about him, and presently he saw a little hut and outside it an oven made of bricks. And there, sweeping out the oven with their hands, were three old witches.

"Good-day, witches!" said the prince. "I've brought you a little broom made of twigs. You'd better clean out your oven with that."

"Hek! Hek! Hek!" croaked the three witches. Each had a hump on her back, and each had a long hooked nose which nearly met her chin. "Hek! hek! hek! Where are you off to?" asked one in a high voice. And, "Hek! hek! hek! What is your business?" asked another in a low voice. And, "Hek! hek! hek! What are you seeking?" asked the third in a voice which was neither high nor low, but a little bit of both.

"Oh," said the prince, "I'm going to seek a bride whose hair is as golden as orange peel, whose skin is as white as orange blossom, and whose temper is as sweet as orange juice!"

"Hek! hek! hek!" croaked the three witches. "Before you find her you'll have to pass the dogs. Give them this loaf of bread, and they'll let you pass. Hek! hek! hek!"

The prince bowed gravely. "Thank you, witches," said he, and he took the loaf of bread and went on his way.

He had not gone very far before he heard a low growling (Grrr!) and a high yelping (Wow-wow!) and a gruff barking (Wuff-wuff!), and in front of him stood three dogs, showing their teeth.

"Good day, dogs!" said the prince, "I've brought you some bread," and he broke the loaf into three pieces and gave each one a portion.

You should have seen them lick their chops and wag their tails.

"Wow-wow! wuff! Where are you going to, prince?"

"Ah!" said the prince. "I'm going to seek a bride whose hair is as

golden as orange peel, whose skin is as white as an orange blossom, and whose temper is as sweet as orange juice."

The dogs sat still and wagged their tails. "Wow-wow, wuff! Before you find *her*, you'll have to pass the gate with the rusty hinges, so you had better take this oil with you."

The prince bowed gravely. "Thank you, dogs," said he, taking the oil, and sure enough he soon came to a gate with rusty hinges. He poured the oil over the hinges, the gate opened and he walked in. "Stop a bit! Stop a bit!" said the gate. "Where are you off to?"

The prince gave his usual answer, and was going on when the gate called out, "If you want a bride like *that,* you had better climb the stairs and take the three oranges which you will find in a bag hanging on a nail. Only be careful! Oh, be very careful, because the old woman who lives up in that tower has a son who is an ogre, and if he sees you he will eat you up!"

The prince bowed. "Thank you, gate," said he, "I'll remember." And he climbed the stairs and knocked at the door of the tower. For a long time nobody answered. He knocked again, and from far away came a voice,

> "Somebody's standing on the mat!
> Tap, tap, tap! Who is that?
> Is he thin or is he fat?"

"Come along and see!" shouted the prince. "Then you'll know." And presently he heard a shuffle-shuffle-shuffle, and an old woman came to the door. No sooner did she see the prince than she began to cry. "Eh, dearie, dearie, dearie!" she sobbed. "Eh, dearie, dearie! Such a beautiful young man coming to this house to be eaten up!"

"Oh, but I haven't," said the prince. "I've come to seek a bride with hair as golden as orange peel, with skin as white as an orange blossom, and a temper as sweet as orange juice!"

"Eh, dearie, dearie, dearie!" sobbed the old woman. "You'll never live to marry *that* bride, for I hear my son coming now! Hide! Quick!"

She pushed the prince behind a cupboard at the top of the stairs. She was only just in time, for at that very moment the tower began to shake and the stairs began to creak, and there was a great blast of wind and a noise like a fire crackling. It was the ogre, and he was sniffing the air. Snuffle! snuffle! snuffle! with a sound like a storm in the chimney.

"I smell a prince. Bring him out!"

Just as he spoke, the prince seized the bag of oranges behind the door, slipped between the ogre's legs, and ran down the stairs.

"Stop him, gate! Lock him in!" yelled the ogre.

"Not I," said the gate. "He oiled my hinges. Run, prince."

"Stop him dogs! Bite him!" screamed the ogre. "Wow-wow! wuff! Not we," said the dogs. "He gave us bread. Run, prince."

"Stop him, witches! Burn him in your oven!" screeched the ogre.

"Not we," said the witches. "He gave us twigs for our oven. Run, prince!"

The prince ran, and he ran and he ran, until he left tower, ogre, gate, dogs and witches quite out of sight. Then he was so thirsty that he lay down and panted.

"Oh," said he, "how I long for a drink!" Suddenly he remembered the oranges. He took out one and was just going to peel it when it jumped out of his hand and rolled away. He ran after it, but he could not catch it, and at last he gave up the chase and took out the second orange. Then a very curious thing happened. He was just going to bite it when it suddenly spoke, and before he could recover from his astonishment it had turned into a lovely girl! "Give me water, beautiful prince!" said she. "Alas!" said the prince, for there was no water in sight. Then the girl faded away before his eyes and he was left with one orange in the bag.

Feeling rather sad and puzzled, he picked up his staff and went on walking, but before he had gone very far he felt so terribly thirsty and tired that he sat down beside a little stream and began to peel the last orange. He held it as tightly as he could, but he had only stripped off one little bit of peel when the orange jumped out of his hand and spun round twice and became a lovely girl.

"Give me water, beautiful prince!" she said.

The prince dipped his hat into the brook, and kneeling on one knee gave her a drink. As he watched her she grew more and more beautiful, and he noticed that her hair was as golden as orange peel and her skin as white as an orange blossom.

"I am the bride whom you have been seeking," said she.

Then the prince took her in his arms and kissed her.

And, of course, she became his queen and they lived happily ever afterwards, because her temper was as sweet as orange juice.

The Talking Thrush

(Indian)

Before what we call the Industrial Revolution took place in England nearly two hundred years ago, the thrush would have found the cotton industry much more like he finds it in India in this story than you might expect. Then the different operations of spinning, weaving, tailoring and so on were all done, not in large factories and by machines as they are today, but by separate families in their own homes and with hand looms and spinning wheels. A merchant would travel round from cottage to cottage collecting and paying for the finished yarn or cloth and carrying it on to another family for the next stage of manufacture.

Once upon a time there was a thrush who lived in a garden. As it was an Indian garden, there were cotton bushes in it, and the cotton bushes were covered with little pods. When the pods burst and the thrush saw all the lovely soft fluffy cotton, he said, "Oh, what a nice lining that would make for my nest!" and he flew down and took some of it and put it inside his nest.

One day, when he was flying through the village, he stopped outside the hut of a cotton-carder. The cotton-carder was a man who combed away all the knots in the cotton and smoothed out the fluff into little balls. "Dear me," said the thrush, "I should like to have some of those little balls myself." So he went back to the garden and collected some cotton. When he had gathered enough, he flew with it in his beak and stopped at the door of the cotton-carder's hut.

"Good-day, cotton-carder," he said.

"Good-day, birdie! Peace be with you," said the cotton-carder. "Can I do anything for you to-day?"

"Yes, please, cotton-carder," said the thrush. "I've got some cotton. Will you comb out the knots and make it into balls?"

"Of course I will," said the cotton-carder. "Come back again tomorrow, Birdie, and you shall have your balls."

Away flew the thrush, and came back again next morning. "Good-day, birdie, peace be with you," said the cotton-carder. "Here are your balls. I've kept one to pay myself for the time and the work, but all the rest are yours."

Now, if the carder had been a bad man, he might have stolen some of the balls, because he knew the thrush couldn't count. But he was an honest man and would not cheat a little bird, so he gave the thrush all the balls except one.

The thrush flew backwards and forwards until he had carried them to his nest.

The next day he happened to pass another hut in the village. From

the door he heard the sound, "Buzzz-whirrr. Buzzz-whirrr." "What's that?" thought he, and he peeped in, with his little brown head on one side and his bright eyes ready to see everything. And what he saw was a man with a spinning-wheel and a great big heap of cotton-balls beside him.

"Good-day, spinner," said the thrush.

"Good-day, birdie," said the spinner. "Peace be with you. Is there anything I can do for you to-day?"

"Well," said the thrush, "I don't want to give you too much trouble, but I've got some cotton-balls like those, and I *do* so want them to be spun into fine thread. Do you think you'd have time to do that for me?"

"Certainly, birdie, certainly," said the spinner. "You fly home and bring me the balls and I'll have some fine thread ready for you by to-morrow morning. Go in peace."

Away flew the thrush, and soon came back with his balls of cotton. When he returned in the morning there were his balls, all spun into fine thread. "Here you are," said the spinner. "I've kept one for payment because I know you haven't any money." "Are you sure that's enough?" said the thrush. "Oh dear me, yes," said the spinner, and although he knew that the thrush couldn't calculate how much thread ought to be there, he was honest.

The thrush flew home with his fine cotton thread, making all sorts of plans. He was a little tired as he had so much to carry, so presently he alighted on the roof of a house to rest. The little house seemed very quiet, so he peeped over the edge of the roof and in at the open door, and there he saw a man weaving cotton thread into cloth. The weaver looked up, and the tiny bright eyes of the thrush looked into his big brown ones.

"Well, I never!" said the weaver, "if that isn't a thrush with a bundle of thread. Good-day and peace be with you, birdie. What can I do for you today?"

"O my uncle," said the thrush (he thought he ought to be very polite because the weaver was so much older than he was), "could you weave this cotton of mine into a piece of cloth?" "Of course! Of course! Of course!" said the weaver, "but I wonder what a little bird like you wants with a piece of cloth?"

"I'll tell you," said the thrush, and he lifted up his little head and the feathers on his throat quivered when he sang,

"I wear my brown feathers by night and by day,
But I want to look bright and I want to look gay.
The cloth, my dear uncle, you'll easily guess
Is to make me a jacket and make me a dress!"

"Ho! Ho! Ho!" laughed the weaver, "give me your thread, birdie, and I'll weave you the best little bit of cloth that was ever made. And, what's more, I'll give it to the dyer and he'll dye a part of it red and a part of it yellow, and won't you look fine? Off you go and come back in two days."

"Tweet, tweet!" said the thrush, and away he flew in a state of great excitement. He was in such a flutter that he could hardly wait for two days to pass, and when he returned to the weaver's house and saw the little piece of scarlet and yellow cloth, he was so delighted

that he flew up and down, in and out, round and round and from side
to side, sometimes in straight lines, sometimes in circles and sometimes
in wiggle-waggles, till the weaver grew quite giddy and had to ask
him to stop.

"Peace be with you, birdie," said he. "You put my head in a whirl.
Be off to the tailor. Here's your cloth. We've taken a tiny strip as
payment, because we knew you wouldn't have any money."

"You dear, honest uncle," said the little thrush, and he flew away
to the tailor with his piece of cloth done up in a neat parcel.

The tailor happened to be rather busy at that moment. He was
sitting cross-legged in the doorway, with an enormous pair of scissors
by his side and a piece of cotton cloth in his hands. He didn't see the
thrush perching on the top of the door. He was a little deaf, too, so
when the thrush piped "Good-day, tailor!" he did not answer.

"How stupid I am!" said the thrush. "I must sing him a song."
And he began to carol away in his clearest tones:—

"I wear my brown feathers by night and by day!
But I want to look bright and I want to look gay!
And tailor, dear tailor, here's cloth in a packet.
Please make me a dress! Please make me a jacket!"

"Eh? Eh? Eh? What's that?" said the tailor. "I'm rather hard of
hearing." The shrill tones of the thrush piped again,

"Oh, tailor, dear tailor, here's cloth in a packet.
Please make me a dress! Please make me a jacket!"

"Well, I never!" said the tailor, "if it isn't a little brown thrush.
Peace be with you, birdie. So you want a dress and a jacket. Give me
your parcel, and I'll see what I can do."

The thrush dropped the packet into the tailor's lap, and the tailor
set to work with needle and thread, and in about half an hour he had
made a lovely little yellow tunic and a red jacket. "Here you are,
birdie!" said he, and he helped the thrush into the little garments.
"You needn't pay me," he said, "because I know you haven't got any
money. Just you sing me a song instead."

"Delighted," trilled the thrush, and he hopped on to the top of
the door and sang,

> "I used to wear feathers by night and by day,
> But I longed to look bright and I longed to look gay.
> And now in my jacket and tunic of yellow
> I'm not a dull bird, but a bright little fellow."

And away he flew, singing, "Thank you! Thank you! Thank you!"
He was so happy that he could not help wanting to look at himself,
so he flew to the king's garden, where there was a clear pool of water
surrounded by shady trees. He perched on one of the low branches
and gazed at his reflection, and was so pleased with what he saw that
he began to sing and sing as though he could never stop.

The king and the queen happened to be walking in the garden just
then, and when they heard the thrush singing, they looked about
until they saw him in the tree.

"Ha-ha-ha!" laughed the queen, and "Ho-ho-ho" laughed the king.
"Peace be with you, birdie! Where did you get your clothes?"

"Sweet-sweet!" said the queen, "pretty dick! Come here and let me
look at you." She stretched out her hand, and the thrush flew down
and perched on her finger. "Oh," said the queen to the king, "*do* look
at the bird's jacket and tunic! I would like to keep them for myself,
just to look at."

"Well," said the king, "keep them if you want them." And he seized
the poor little thrush and pulled off its new clothes and gave them
to the queen.

"Please! Please!" said the thrush, "give me back my jacket and tunic
—they're much too small for you,

"I used to wear feathers by night and by day,
But I want to look bright and I want to look gay.
This is the *first time* that I've ever heard
Of a king and a queen being cruel to a bird!"

"Nonsense!" said the king crossly, "don't be silly. If you talk like
that I shall cook you in a pie and eat you up."

"But it's true," said the thrush.

"Oh, very well then," said the king, "I *will* eat you up!" and he seized the thrush by its fluffy feathers.

"Oh-ho!" said the thrush; "the king pulls out fluff like a cotton-carder—but he's not so honest."

The king took no notice, but carried the little bird into the kitchen and put it inside a pie-dish which he then covered with dough. Then he began to cut and shape the dough into a pattern.

"Snip-snap! Snip-snap!" sang the thrush. "The king cuts like a tailor—but he's not so honest."

"You be quiet!" said the king, and he popped the pie into the oven, while the little thrush snuggled down and cheeped with joy, because it was as cosy and warm as a nest.

When the king opened the oven door again and saw that the piecrust was nice and brown, he pulled out the dish and, being a very greedy man, swallowed the pie *whole!*

"Sweet, sweet, sweet!" piped the thrush inside the king. "The king's just like any other man inside—but he's not so honest."

The king looked a little nervous, but he said nothing. He went into his hall and began to talk to some grand gentlemen of his court, but no sooner had he finished speaking than a little voice inside him piped out, "Ha-ha! The king's just like any other man inside—but he's not so honest."

The gentlemen looked at one another, and then at the king. The king, of course, was *most* embarrassed, so he pretended that nothing unusual had happened, but that he had rather a bad cough. "Aha, ahem-ahem!" coughed the king.

"The king's just like any other man inside—but he's not so honest," piped the thrush louder than ever. At last the gentlemen of the court began to laugh, and the king grew very angry; but the angrier he grew, the louder piped the thrush, "The king's just like any other man inside —but he's not so honest!"

Now the king was furious. He stamped his foot and he dashed from the room and went straight to bed. But it was no use. Whenever he turned on his pillow the thrush began to pipe.

This went on for days. Even when the king was in his council chamber, talking to his wise men, up piped the thrush, saying, "The king's just like any other man inside—but he's not so honest," and all the wise men laughed and laughed.

At last the king sent for the doctor. "What is the matter with your Majesty?" asked the doctor. But before the king had time to answer, a voice sang out, "The king's just like any other man inside—but he's not so honest!"

"Doctor!" shouted the king. "TAKE OUT THAT BIRD!"

The doctor frowned. "Sire," he said, "I'll do my best. Open your mouth."

So the king opened his mouth.

"Wider," said the doctor.

And the king opened it wider.

"Wider still!" shouted the doctor.

And the king opened his mouth so wide that his face looked like a big, oval-shaped hole. The doctor peeped inside. "Peace be with you, birdie!" he whispered. "Out you come!"

In a few minutes there was a little flutter of wings and out flew the thrush. And he had the impudence to perch on top of the king's head and sing,

> "I'll never look bright and I'll never look gay,
> For I'm going to wear feathers by night and by day.
> My dear little jacket was stolen away
> By a king who's like everyone else is, inside!
> But he isn't so honest, I know, 'cause I've tried!"

With that the thrush flew away and nobody ever saw him again.

As for the greedy king, well, you can guess what everybody thought about him.

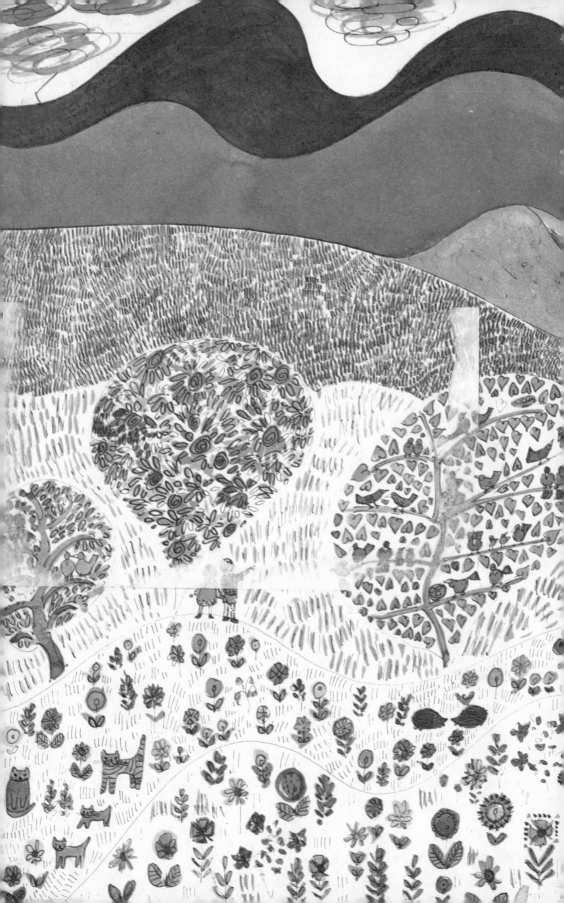